ISBN-13: 9789354161780

Cover design by: Lansingliu Rose Pamei

TALES OF THE ZELIANGRONG NAGA

Ahmang, Niumaduan, Dithuailu

and many more...

Compiled & Annotated

by

Lansingliu Rose Pamei, MSW

Editor: Fr George Menamparampil, sdb

DEDICATION

This compilation is dedicated to my Mum and Dad who have always been my source of strength and inspiration. I thank them for their unconditional love, support and prayers all through my life. May God continue to shower them with all they need.

Mr and Mrs John Didah Pamei

CONTENTS

ACKNOWLEDGEMENTS

Most of the tales in this volume were narrated to me by the folks of Old Tamenglong, Manipur. Our interactions and the time we spent together were very special and so much fun. Helping me in this collection right from the start was my cousin Singamliu Newmei, who gave me all the support I required during our visits to the village and the chats with the elders. I appreciate her selflessness, genuine concern and all her good will for the success of this venture. I take pride in mentioning all those elders of Old Tamenglong who gave me their time:

Lunguangreiyang pei

Keiramphuiyang pu

R.K. Khangbuiyang

Namrichuang

Late Namphun pei

Late Tiuriangliu Panmei

Late Kungdiuwang pou

Late Kungdiuwang pei

Special thanks to my confidant Jianpui Khumba, my aunt Guitiuliu Panmei, my family and friends for motivating me to complete this compilation. I hope the stories delight everyone and prove to be a step forward in the effort towards conservation of our folklores.

Elders, repositories of our cultural heritage
(Pic: Old Tamenglong, Manipur)

PREFACE

The ethnonym 'Zeliangrong' refers to a cognate community of kindred Naga tribes namely Zeme, Liangmei, Rongmei and Npuimei; the nomenclature being derived from the first syllable of the names of the three larger tribes, viz 'Ze' from Zeme, 'Liang' from Liangmei and 'Rong' from Rongmei. The nomenclature was first coined at a conference of representatives of the kindred tribes on 15 February 1947 at Keishamthong Imphal, Manipur, with the objective of strengthening lineage fraternity and unity, and facilitating cooperation in all aspects of development.

Let me attempt to present here what I have received, conceived and fathomed on the genesis of this mystic community.

Legends narrate that it was God who created the first Man in the form of a boy named Puakrei or Dirannang, and the first Woman in the form of a girl named Dichalu. To protect them from evils and the wild, God hid the boy and girl in a cave, the entrance to which was covered by a large stone. But, a bovine bull (mithun) rolled away the stone by its horns and the innocent boy and girl came out of the cave to begin human life on earth. It is told that the two grew up in innocence as brother and sister, unconcerned even about their nudity.

However, as they grew up, inspired by God, the boy felt that they should marry; but marriage was not possible as siblings. So, he thought out a plan. They had to become as though belonging two different clans between whom marriage is allowed. Puakrei told Dichalu that he would go behind a hill and unexpectedly come running towards her. She should then call out to him, 'Apou' (form of addressing an elder male of other clans, practised till today) instead of 'Achai' (elder brother).

For the first seven times they tried it out, Dichaliu instinctively addressed him "Achai". Upon his insistence, on the eighth round, she addressed him as "Apou". From then on, the boy no longer treated her as his sister, and consequently, they were united as the first couple on earth. As time passed, they were blessed with four sons, namely Nguiba (Nguibou), Sagee, Aneiu-wa and Chatiu. While Nguiba is recognized as the forefather of the Zeliangrong, the other three sons are recognized as the forefathers of the other Naga tribes.

In course of their migrations in search of food and shelter, many ethnic groups of the Nagas coming from different directions converged at a place called Makhel, a location considered as the original abode of the Nagas. It is a village in the present-day district of Senapati in Manipur, India. After many years of co-existence at Makhel a grand dispersal took place. The various tribesmen belonging to the Zeliangrong, Mao, Poumai, Angami, Lotha, Maram, Tangkhul, Thangal, Sema, Chakeshang, etc., moved out, each to their own area.

At the time of the dispersal, to record this momentous event, they erected a stone Megalith and planted the tree now known as Chutebu. They also took an oath to reunite at this place at some time in the future. T.C Hodson mentions this in 1911, "At Makhel is to be seen a stone now erect which marks the place from which the common ancestor (of the Nagas) emerged from the earth. Makhel is regarded as the centre from where the migration took place."

From Makhel, the sons of Nguiba, the ancestors of the Zeliangrong people, went westward and took temporary shelter at Nrimrengdi, then at Ramting Kabin and Chawang Phungning and finally came to occupy Makuilongdi or Nkuilongdi meaning "Big round mountain", which till today is considered the mother ground of the Zeliangrong community.

Legends have it that, Nguiba had two wives and three sons. When his first wife was issueless, he married his second. After his second wife bore him his first son, Kadingbou, his first wife bore him his second son, Magangtubou/Namgang. Thereafter, his second wife bore him his third son, Rembangbe (Nriengbangbe or Rengbangbou).

It is said that after Nguiba died, Kadingbou, his eldest son, succeeded him as the chief of the vast land and Makuilongdi rapidly progressed to the point when it had 7777 (Seven thousand seven hundred and seventy-seven) households. Beyond that point, various challenges such as overpopulation, scarcity of resources in the vicinity, etc., culminated in a famine. Legends tell us that it was a curse for over-lavish living and disregard of the rules of nature. This disaster forced the descendants of Nguiba to disperse in different directions. Kadingbou and his followers stayed behind in Makuilongdi and the surrounding area and subsequently came to be called the Liangmai, meaning the 'Northern settlers'. Magangtubou/Namgang and his followers went to Ramzengning (valley) and became the Zeme, derived from the word

Mejahme (dwellers of the warmer or lower region). Rembangbe with a large number of followers went Southward to Kamarongbojam (empty land) and came to be known as Marongmei or Rongmei, (meaning dwellers of the fallow or empty lands and of the Southern region). The Rongmei and Npuimei, another group of descendants of Nguiba who went to the South-Eastern part, settled at Kajinglong for many generations and consider it their original native village.

Today, the constituent ethnic units of the Zeliangrong, which earlier included the Puimei, are recognized under the Indian Constitution as individual indigenous tribes: Zeme, Liangmei, Rongmei, Kabui and Npuimei. They inhabit the tri-junction of Assam, Manipur and Nagaland in India.

It is only rather recently that these tribes were exposed to the world beyond them vis-à-vis introduction to a formal education system, the market economy, etc., The only method of 'documentation' among the community was transmission by word of mouth. Hence, historical and factual data to authenticate the actual origin of the race are not available. However, mentions of the race under different names are found in the records of the erstwhile Kingdom of Manipur and limited works of some historians and research scholars of the twentieth century.

I refrain from attempting to delve into or even summarize in this area. Within this present context, suffice it to say that the existence of similar or near-similar myths, legends, fables and folklore, handed down through generations among the various constituent units of the cognate community of the Zeliangrong including the Npui-mei, the prevalence of many common words in the various languages of the individual tribes, and the common reference that traditional ritual practices make even today to the cave as the place where human life began, point strongly to their common ancestor Nguiba, Puak-rei, and ultimately to the Supreme Being, God.

The beauty of myths, legends, fables and folklores, is that they convey in the simplest form, themes, messages or values to warn or improve human society. These themes, messages or values that flow naturally from the stories are intended to educate, form and discipline the young. They attempt to deter them from practices that are harmful to society; they impart knowledge of nature; they transmit the community's history; they develop a love for the socio-cultural practices of the tribe; and they encourage the inculcation of the same. In these stories you will experience once again the ancient practice of all cultures: to include a mystic setting of time and space; to revolve events around a Supreme God, Universe and Man; to have witches and wizards mingling with man; to make all other forms of life talk to man; and to spin magic spells, boons and curses. You will get the "Happily ever after" type of stories and the tragic ending "Romeo-Juliet" type of stories. These are spices that arouse taste and facilitate propagation.

While many are based on partial truths, an equal number or more of such narrations have no factual basis and are creations of a powerful imagination. These narrations have in common the fact that they do not have authors and they normally end with some theme, message or moral. However, in my perception, because they were handed down for generations only by word of mouth, they are subject to the risk of duplication, distortion, dilution, discontinuity and even adulteration to suit certain fancies of the narrator. Even if nothing of these is intentionally done, it is absolutely normal and totally expected that there are dozens of versions of these same stories. Disputes about which version is the correct one or the best one would be totally pointless.

It is here that putting these narrations into forms other than oral should be encouraged. A few works have been documented and even digitalized. Since mid-1990's, picturization of many of the Zeliangrong folktales has been done in film formats.

This compilation of some of the Tales of Zeliangrong by Ms Rose Pamei is lovingly dedicated to the beautiful daughter-parents relationship of her family. It is a great contribution, not only to the younger generations of these tribes, but also to story-lovers everywhere. Without such written collections, they would miss them. Through circumstances more than by choice, children today do not have the luxury and the joys of listening to bedtime stories from parents and grandparents. Older children and adults who can read, can now put their hands on books like this one and cherish the myths, legends, fables and folklore of their forefathers.

I express my sincere appreciation to Ms Lansingliu Rose Pamei MSW and the editor of the compilation, Rev. Fr. M.C. George SDB, for this contribution to enrich the Zeliangrong Society and the cultural heritage of humanity.

I wish you 'HAPPY READING!'

Dr. Stephen Kamson MBBS,
IRHS Senior Divisional Medical Officer
Northeast Frontier Railway, India

FORWARD

Folklores help us understand and love our own identity and culture, and respect and accept the cultures of others we associate with. We are proud of all that defines our identity and we are proud to have neighbours and compatriots who have equally rich and beautiful folklore and cultural heritage.

At times our folk knowledge determines our decisions and opinions. The popular beliefs and customs of the Zeliangrong Naga tribes, like those of everyone else, have evolved over the decades and centuries through their transmission from one generation to the next through oral recounting. In the process, the stories that were earlier the same or very similar have become, in some cases, quite distinct one from the other, though with strong similarities.

In this volume the tale of "Ahmang" tells us that the concept of Master-Servant relationship did not exist in traditional Naga society. The attitude of equality of all humans is at the root of Naga Culture. In the story, Ahmang took two servants after he became prosperous. On the day of the grand celebration for his Tarangkai, he realized that using his two helpers as servants at the party would have meant that he was going against tradition. One sees that there is no concept of high or low in a tribal society. Not wanting his guests to see that he was going against the noble tradition of his people, he sent one of his servants away to the field. The other was given a task in the house.

(Tarangkai is a traditional house of the Zeliangrong Naga tribe. It cannot be built by just anyone, but by someone who has wealth, power and prestige. It is built with just one middle pillar which should be very high. Usually all the villagers have to be involved in the building of a Tarangkai. Many varieties of animals are sacrificed to appease the supernatural and the villagers involved in the construction are fed by the owner till the final house-warming ceremony.)

Women were valued and respected among the Zeliangrong Nagas. Beauty and talents are highly regarded in women as are 'power and strength' in men. In traditional Zeliangrong Naga culture, a bride is not given away without a price. We see this in the tale of "Ahmang" where the orphan went seeking for his aunt's price even after many years. The extraordinary beauty and talent of "Dithuailu" is talked about even today.

The mention of 'dormitory' for unmarried men and women *(known as khangchiu for men and kailiu for women)* in many of our folk tales is simply an undeniable evidence that our Zeliangrong Naga Community loved social life and community living even in the past.

(The 'dormitory' was a place where the unmarried boys and girls came together usually at night for social purposes. It was owned and maintained by the village head. A leader would be appointed from among the boys and girls. Once married, a person could not be a part of it anymore. Their association usually led to the youths choosing their life partners from within the group itself. It was more like a learning and entertainment centre. The youths learned the values of the tribe, its traditions as well as crafts and skills related to household

chores, social skills, battle tactics for boys, etc. Games and sports, music, dance and social life were its main ingredients.)

The practice of community work by youths on special occasions and taking turns to go to each other's fields were healthy practices depicting the helping and warm nature of the Zeliangrong Naga tribal. Our folklores also mention certain taboos in our society. Some such taboos were: the purification before entering a house after a funeral, heading back home from fields before the sun sets, involving the whole village when hunting big animals. When a marriage was to take place outside the home village, people had to make the journey to the place of marriage in a single day and not halt anywhere for a night on the way. The dead had to be buried the very same day they passed away. Folklore refers to such taboos and rules as perfectly normal practices.

On the other hand, we see evidence in the folktales of evils like jealousy, corruption, cruelty to orphans by society, illicit relationships, ostracism of certain people from the community, abuse of children by stepparents, etc.

The tales of "Rokheang" and "Ahmang", among many others, show how the society treated orphans. Ostracism used to be practised in many villages and is believed to exist till today in some form or the other in some very interior parts of the state. In this volume one finds it mentioned in the "Beautiful Spinters" where the two young girls decided to leave the village on their own because they were thought to be vampires. They were left with no choice because no one accepted them. Other reasons for 'ostracism' could be diseases like leprosy. We tend to follow fads and trends blindly not knowing their implications and what our best interests are. This practice may cause us more harm than good. We cannot and are not expected to live our life today as the folks in our folklore lived; however, neither should we despise or totally ignore all elements found in our traditions. We retain the good ones and modify the ones that do not suit the present day.

Not much of the Zeliangrong folklore is recorded in writing. However, the richness of 'art and culture' does not depend entirely on its scripting and documentation. We can still be 'truly civilized' by retaining the traditional values with refinement in our thought, manners and taste.

I sincerely hope that reading these stories gives you at least a little of the great pleasure I experienced while collecting them.

I would be glad to take note of your comments and suggestions when I revise this collection for any eventual subsequent edition.

Lansingliu Rose Pamei

A DOG ON THE MOON

How the dog landed up on the moon

Have you ever observed the moon and contemplated that there is something mysterious about it? Here's what our folks had to say.

It is a belief of humanity even today that unseen forces always come to the rescue of the oppressed. This tale is one of such wherein, the treatment meted out to the young boy turned out to be a blessing in disguise.

Once upon a time there lived five brothers. All five of them would work in the fields of the family. The youngest was named Aneuwang. As he was the youngest among the five boys, he would go to the field just to help his brothers. He was assigned the task of cooking for his four elder brothers, while they did whatever was required for the crops.

They had built a little shelter of straw, leaves and bamboo where they could cook their food, take rest and eat their meals. Aneuwang would gather firewood, collect water, and cook for them; a task they considered much easier than theirs. They presumed it to be easier for there was a stream that flowed just by the side of the field and there was no shortage of firewood lying around.

One afternoon, Aneuwang took a container and went over to the stream to collect water. On his way back he saw a snake. The natural instinct was to kill it before it bit anyone. So, he put his water pot down, grabbed a stone and killed the snake. He stood there for a while just to be sure that the snake was dead. But then, to his surprise another snake appeared. It might have been the partner of the one he had killed. It saw that its friend was dead. It turned around and went away as though it was trying to avoid suffering the same fate. Aneuwang watched the snake slithering back into the bushes.

As he picked up his container to get back to his work, he was in for another surprise; the snake was back. What was even more astonishing, it held a leaf in its mouth. He was fascinated by the sight and stood there wonder-struck, staring at the snake without disturbing it. The live snake crawled to its dead mate and laid the leaf gently by its side. After a while, the dead snake gave a shudder, came alive and the two of them slid away into the bushes.

Aneuwang was so caught up in this adventure with the snakes that he did not realize the passing of time. He had forgotten all about his job of cooking food for his brothers. It was already time for the afternoon meal. His brothers came to the little shelter in the field, all hungry and ready for food. Finding that there was no food ready, they got furious with him and beat him up. Aneuwang was hurt badly.

The wound hurt him very much, but there was little he could do about it. He hated his brothers anyway, but there were four of them and they were much bigger than he was. He was now furious with his brothers for the beating he had received. He decided to leave them and run far away from home. But his wounds were serious and it would be foolish to move out of the security and care in his home in such a condition. For a while he was in despair as he did not want to spend another minute with his cruel brothers.

Then he remembered the snakes. He realized that there must have been something special, even miraculous about the leaves that had brought the dead snake back to life. He wondered whether they could heal his wounds, too.

He went back to the place where he had killed the snake and searched around for the special leaf. He found it and took it with him to identify the tree or plant from which it had been plucked. He peeled out a layer of the bark of the tree and touched all his body with it. His wounds were healed instantly. He peeled off some more bark of the 'life giving tree' and took it with him. With all his wounds now fully cured, he set out immediately for a village nearby. He did not want to be with his brothers ever again.

He walked and walked the jungle alone and, along the footpath leading to a village, he came across the body of a dead dog that someone must have thrown out. He thought he would try out the magical power of the 'life giving tree' he had discovered. He took the bark of the tree and touched the dog with it. The dog immediately came back to life. Now he had a new companion. He took the dog along with him and went on towards the village. He reached the nearest village and halted for the night at an old lady's place. He stayed with her for a few days.

One afternoon he heard people crying in the village. He asked the old lady, "What is wrong with the people?" The lady replied, "People are grieving the death of a girl." Having had the experience of bringing the dog back to life, Aneuwang wanted to try the special bark on the dead girl too. He said to the old lady, "I can bring the dead girl back to life. Please take me to her parents." The lady was not convinced but she did not react negatively. Without questioning much of what Aneuwang had said, she led him to the house of the deceased. He walked up straight to the girl's father and said, "Do not be distressed. I can bring your daughter back to life, if you let me marry her." The father happily agreed to his proposal.

Aneuwang asked everyone to leave the room. Then he

touched the girl with the bark of the healing tree. At once the girl opened her eyes and sat up. Her parents were then called in to the room. When they saw her awake, they were extremely happy. They had no problem whatever to give her hand in marriage to him. Aneuwang took his wife and moved on to another village to settle down there. The two of them made a beautiful couple. They worked hard and loved each other. Three little sons were born to them.

He had never told anyone about the healing tree. He kept the tree's bark in a box so that no one would find it. He would only tell his wife very frequently not to open the box. His wife wondered why her husband repeated these instructions of his so very often. She thought there must be something very precious in the box. Since her husband took so great care of it, she was equally curious to know what exactly it contained.

One day, when her husband was away, she opened the box and found the bark of the healing tree. It was moist and was covered with fungus since it was kept closed up in the box from the time it was peeled off the tree. "What is the use of keeping this?" she thought. However, she could sense it was precious to her husband since he was so very particular about protecting it. She took it out and spread it on the ground outside to dry it in the sun and prevent it from rotting.

Their dog, the same one that Aneuwang had brought back to life, saw the bark lying outside and took it back inside. Aneuwang's wife saw it and thought the dog was playing with the bark. She was afraid he would chew up the bark, tear it and spoil it. She took it out again and put it back in the sun. The dog picked it up again and took it back inside the house. It seemed as though the dog had sensed the danger in the bark getting exposed to the sun. The dog in fact was trying to protect the bark and prevent it from drying up.

Since Aneuwang's wife did not understand this, she would keep taking it out. This went on for quite some time. Alas, the Sun and Moon saw the bark of the healing tree lying out there on the ground in front of the house. Both the celestial bodies wanted it for itself. They came swooping down as fast as they could to grab it. The dog saw them coming and started barking at them. It tried to prevent the sun and the moon from taking the bark away. It snatched the bark, bit down hard on it and tried to take it inside. The moon was the faster of the two attackers. She managed to get a hold on one end of the bark. The dog would not let go off it and bit down on it even harder. The moon flew back up to its own place in the sky with the dog hanging on to the other end of the bark as he would not leave it.

When Aneuwang returned home, he saw the box lying open and asked his wife what had happened. His wife confessed to her mistake and all that had happened. Aneuwang did not want to lose his precious bark that had saved his life and earned him his beautiful wife. He wanted to get it back regardless of what it would cost him.

He invited all living beings on earth to help him build a tower that would reach up to the moon in the sky. He said to them, "The Moon has taken away something that can restore life to the dead. Let us get it back."

All living things pitched in enthusiastically. They realized that none of them would ever need to die any more if they could get back what the moon had stolen from Aneuwang. They collected the best building materials from all over the earth. They worked hard on the tower and gradually they were approaching the sky. They abandoned all their personal work and struggled together, thinking only of the eternal life they would have if they could only bring the 'life giving bark' back from the moon. The tower stood tall and it almost reached the sky.

The termites saw the tower and they were not happy. They had not been invited to be a part of the mission. Aneuwang might have thought they were too small and incapable of contributing much to the project. Unseen by anyone, the little creatures set their jaws to all the pillars of the mighty tower, sending it crashing back to the earth. All the other beings were discouraged by this misfortune and did not have the courage to start building a new tower all over again.

And that is why, even today, if you look up at the moon you will see a dog sitting there, perhaps still hanging on to the bark in its teeth. It is believed that a healing and life-restoring plant once existed on the earth. It was taken away by the moon and people continue to die even today. On the other hand, considering the tiny termites as insignificant due to their appearance had cost mankind very dearly.

AHMANG
Rags to Riches

◆ ◆ ◆

Long ago, when animals and humans used to co-exist in peace and communicated with each other, the child Ahmang was born to a couple in a place called Taning, now in Nagaland. His parents left him orphaned when he was very young. He migrated towards Churachandpur, currently located in Manipur. Ahmang had no friends. People did not like him because he was an orphan and very poor. He was alone all the time and did not grow up like any other normal child surrounded by peers. The people of those times used to treat all orphans cruelly. They were considered to have been the cause of the untimely death of their parents. Innocent children suffered. It was difficult for them to survive, despised as they were by everyone.

Ahmang's parents had not left him any fields. He was so poor that he did not have seeds to sow or even a knife. One day he decided that he was old enough to start working. He would make a farm of his own. But from where would he get seeds to sow? He said to himself, "I will catch a few birds that feed on someone's harvest. Let me kill the birds, extract the seeds from their stomach and use them as seeds for my field." He went to a paddy field nearby and set traps for the birds. Only one bird got caught in one of his traps.

He took the bird, cut its throat and took out all the food grains. He did not throw its feathers outside because he was afraid people would accuse him of stealing someone's chicken. Instead, he hid the feathers under his bed. The next day Ahmang heard some noise under his bed that sounded like the clanging of metal objects. He investigated the source of the noise and found that the bird's feathers had turned into a knife. He badly needed a knife to clear the jungle with, so that he could start cultivating his crops.

He took the knife and went to the jungle. He soon found that it was not an ordinary knife. When he cut just one tree, a whole portion of the jungle was cleared of all trees and bushes. The cleared area was sufficient for him to start his jhum cultivation. When the ground was ready, he sowed the seeds that he had collected from the bird's throat. To his surprise the seeds did not sprout and grow as paddy but as gourds. Ahmang had no complaints. "Whatever God has given me, let me make the best of it," he thought. Villagers saw his field and laughed at the gourd plants. They said among themselves, "Why is this stupid boy planting gourds instead of paddy? What will he do with it?"

Ahmang himself did not know what he would do with all his gourds. However, he took great care of them. He joined a group of young people who took turns to work in each other's fields. When the turn came to work in Ahmang's field, his companions removed all the gourd plants and left only the weeds behind. It left him so devastated that he was once again left with nothing. "What do I do now? Even the gourd plants are gone," he said to himself. He did not have the courage to tell his colleagues that they were doing something wrong, that he wanted the gourds to stay and the weeds to be pulled out. He was just an orphan and it was his fate to bear all the ill-treatment and humiliations from everyone.

There was just one gourd plant left in his field that had not been pulled out. His friends had not noticed it for it grew near the fence, in a corner. The plant grew big and covered the whole of his farm. That single plant bore thousands of fruits, too. In order to store the gourds, he built a barn. He became a 'laughing stock' for his friends. Some even asked him, "Where is your paddy? Are you going to store gourds in a barn? They will only rot in there!" Others murmured to themselves, "What will poor Ahmang store in the barn?"

A kind, gentle-hearted lady passed by and saw Ahmang working hard. She took pity on him and asked, "What are you doing my boy?" Ahmang replied, "I am building a barn to store whatever is available on my farm." "Good work, my dear boy. A barn can be useful for many other things, too," she said and went away. Not long after, harvest season arrived, and he collected the gourds inside his barn. When he broke one, he found that it was filled with food grains. He hastily took them all inside and broke them one by one. In no time his barn was filled with grains. No one in the village had as much paddy as he had.

Since he had enough food grains, he wanted to build a special house for himself, known as a 'Tarangkai.' In order to make preparations for the task, he decided to go to his aunt's house to ask his uncle, his aunt's husband, for her bride price. It had not yet been given to her family of which he was the lone survivor now.

(For a man to ask for a woman's hand in marriage, the man has to pay a price to the woman's family. It is usually given in kind in the form of cattle, food grains, money or ornaments. It may be paid immediately, at the time of marriage, or even many years after the marriage.)

Since he was poor, he could not prepare any special dishes to offer his uncle as a gift. He collected the bones of animals. He cooked some of these and took the dish to his aunt's place. When he arrived, his aunt was there. She asked him, "Why are you here, my son?" He replied, "I came here to ask for your bride price." Handing over what he had brought he said, "This is what I have brought for your husband." His aunt opened the package and saw that he had cooked the bones of animals. She took it outside, careful not be seen by anyone, and threw it away. She then took out the best meat available in the house and cooked it for him.

She packed it up, handed it over to Ahmang and said, "Listen to me, son! When my husband comes, tell him that you have brought this food for him. My husband will tell you to ask whatever you want. He may even suggest several things you could ask for. But do not accept anything. Ask only for this piece of rope that is hanging here." It was a rope that was used to tie cattle with. Ahmang did exactly as he had been advised by his aunt. He was offered cattle, food grains, ornaments, etc. But he did not accept any of them. Pointing to the rope that was hanging in the corner of the house, he said, "I want only a small piece of that rope and nothing more." So, his uncle cut a piece of the rope and gave it to him.

His aunt knew exactly what to do with the piece of rope. She put it into his basket along with waste and dry leaves. She then instructed him, "Do not remove these dry leaves and waste until you reach home. When you reach there, build a fence with lots of space inside. Then take out the piece of rope and cut it into as many pieces as possible."

Ahmang did not understand why his aunt gave him such weird instructions. "What can I do with all these waste leaves?" he thought. He had no clue what would happen. On his way back, he looked at the dry leaves and waste in his basket and tried to throw it away. Each time he tried to do so, there would come up a mighty wind as in a big storm. So, he put everything back in the basket and proceeded on his journey. As he had been told by his aunt, he built a fence around a large area of land. He cut the rope into as many pieces as possible and scattered them within the fenced area. To his surprise, the next day he found the pieces of rope had turned into cattle.

The cattle grew day by day and some of them would escape out of the fence because there was not enough space inside it. Those that came out of the fence became the property of evil spirits. In a short while, Ahmang became a very rich man. It was then time for him to build his special house (Tarangkai). As per tradition, a Tarangkai is symbolic and is built only by someone with status and wealth. On the occasion of the inauguration of his Tarangkai he invited to his grand feast, not only all the people of his village, but all the animals and birds of the forest. It was a grand celebration.

A festive occasion, Old Tamenglong

Many animals and birds prepared themselves to attend the party. The Hornbill asked the Owl, "Are you not going to the party?" The owl replied, "I do not have good looks as you have. Let me not go to the party and embarrass myself." Hornbill said, "Do not worry, my friend. I will hide you under my wings."

The Owl agreed to go along and both of them proceeded to the party. All who were gathered there saw the Hornbill approaching and exclaimed, "What a beautiful bird! This will be the king of the birds!" Hearing them, the Hornbill got excited. It forgot all about the Owl that was hidden under its wings. It flapped its wings harder and wider and the Owl fell off. Everyone then commented, "This bird was hiding something. He cannot be the king."

A Hornbill

The Kite and Rat were also busy doing their make-up in preparation for the grand celebration. They helped each other in beautifying themselves. The Rat decorated the tail of the Kite. It cut off all the unnecessary feathers and made it look groomed and beautiful. It took a lot of time to get the kite all spruced up and they were running quite behind their schedule before they got around to decorating the Rat's tail. So the Kite said, "We are getting late. It is easiest to make your tail perfectly round." It rolled the tail of the Rat. This is how, a rat's tail remains perfectly round till today.

The Rat was not pleased with the way his tail looked. He was angry and said to himself, "Just wait and see what I will do to you." But the Rat never got the chance to take revenge on the bird. Till today, Kites and Rats are great enemies. They cannot bear the sight of each other. Both of them reached right on time for the party. When they arrived, everyone saw the beauty of the Kite. They all declared, "The Kite should be the king of the birds."

The Flea and the Hare also decided to go together. Since the Flea smells bad he had not been too keen on attending the party. But he was persuaded to go by the Hare and they agreed to hide each other's shortcomings. When they reached Ahmang's Tarangkai everyone began murmuring, "What a bad smell! Whose smell is this?" The Hare replied, "It is my friend's smell." The Flea felt very embarrassed by this and went away. It waited for the Hare to return from the party so that it could take its revenge.

The main celebration was about to begin. Someone inquired, "Has everyone arrived, including all the animals and birds?" "Not yet. A man and the Tiger have not yet arrived," someone from the crowd answered. After some time, the Tiger and the man appeared. The Tiger came first followed by the man. Since they had not come together, everyone decided that Man and Tiger could not be friends nor equals. "Men shall fear Tigers during the night, and Tigers will fear men during the day," suggested the crowed. From that day on, both have power over each other half of each day.

As the party progressed, a serious issue came up for discussion, "How should the nodes in a bamboo be arranged?" The Toad suggested, "If it has to have a node, let the whole tree be filled solid as though with one continuous node. If that is not possible, let it be hollow throughout without a single node." Everyone thought this did not sound like a good idea. They pinched the Toad for coming up with something so stupid. So, the Toad's back remains rough even till today. The Robin then opined,

"Let the bamboo tree have as many nodes as it needs and be hollow between every pair of nodes." Everyone thought this was an excellent idea. They patted the Robin on its back. Since everyone at the party patted the Robin – and there so many guests at this party – the bird became very small and remains so to this day.

There was another great issue to be settled that night. What names ought to be given to the planets (Sun and the Moon)? Everyone sat in silence because they had absolutely no idea how to go about dealing with this great problem. The Rabbit stood up and said, "Let us call them Sun and Moon." No sooner had he given his opinion than he ran out of the Tarangkai at his usual fast speed. Everyone shouted, "Wait! Wait! Let us all hear your wonderful opinion again." But the Rabbit would not turn back. Someone who had a lump of pig's fat in his hand threw it at the Rabbit. It struck him right on his butt. Hence, even today a rabbit's butt has lots of fat in it.

The bear had also decided to attend the grand event. He was a little late, though, in getting himself ready. When he arrived, everyone was already seated including a tortoise that was stuck against the wall. Someone invited the bear to sit down. Thinking the tortoise to be a wooden seat, he picked it up and gave it to the bear to sit on it. The furious tortoise got up and walked away. It was Ahmang who noticed the tortoise's anger and calmed him down, inviting the animal to stay back and enjoy the rest of the party.

It was, indeed, a very grand party. Ahmang ensured that no one would go away dissatisfied. When the feasting got over, all the animals and birds returned home happily.

Trouble, however, awaited the Hare back home. The Flea was furious with the Hare for the latter had not helped him hide his foul smell as the agreement between them had clearly stipulated. This was a serious breach of trust and the Flea had missed a good part the feast. The feasting was now all done, and it was time for his pound of flesh. The Flea sucked blood from the Hare and spat it out on the roadside. A bird that saw the fresh blood on his way back home said to himself, "Let my feathers be red." He went and soaked itself in the hare's blood. Hence the colour of this bird is usually red even today.

Ahmang wanted to find out whether his guests had been truly satisfied at his party. He disguised himself and waited on the roadside to question all who had come. Everyone replied, "We have never before seen such a grand party in our lives." Varieties of meat and rice wine had been served at the party. Some people had brought their contribution to it – dry-gourd vessels containing the best possible wines. There were others, too, who came, but did not like Ahmang. They had brought along in their gourds the water they had used to soak rice for wine-making. They were confident that no one would make out the difference as the two things have a very similar colour. When they saw that the others had brought their best wines, they felt ashamed of themselves and quietly emptied their gourds, pouring out the waste water at the back of the house. It produced a peculiar musical sound as it was poured out of the guard container. The sound was over-heard by a seasonal insect. It said to itself, "Wow! What a noise! Let me take it as my song." Since then the insect could usually be heard singing that same song when every spring ends.

At the time of this party Ahmang had two servants. They were called Namdiuriang and Khuidiyang. He did not want to treat anyone as servants during the grand celebration. *(The concept of Master-Servant relationship did not exist in traditional Rongmei society. So using his two helpers as servants at the party would have meant that he was going against tradition.)* He sent Namdiuriang off to another village to sell bulls. To Khuidiyang, he said, "You will be in the house during the party. But you must stand there holding a rope to which a bull's head will be tied."

(The bull's head is usually hung at a certain height from the ground. It is like a sport at which strong bachelors of the village compete. They have to jump up and try to catch the animal's head. Whoever gets it by cutting the rope is considered the winner. Since power was associated with physical strength, the winner would be honoured by the villagers.)

A bull mithun

The old folks saw Khuidiyang holding the rope throughout the party. They considered this a useless task for a man. It meant that the man was helpless and useless. The old men composed a song right at the party and sang it. It went,

> "He was no one…. but a rope
>
> A useless man he is;
>
> Though a man,
>
> he cannot be used anywhere else."

Khuidiyang heard the song and felt ashamed of himself. He did not survive for long in the service of Ahmang. He left his master and ran off by himself. Namdiuriang returned home after the party was over and lived with Ahmang happily ever after.

ANGUMA

The gods always have their way

Anguma had many siblings. Being the eldest among the siblings, her mother used to ask her to take care of her younger ones while she went to the field. She would feed them, put them to sleep and wash their clothes. She would see to it that the children did not quarrel or get into fights. She ensured that they do not cry or get dirty. She also did not let them go wandering about where they might not be safe.

One day she took her younger ones to the woods which was near her house. The forest had a wide variety of trees and plants. Among them, there was a big tree that bore very beautiful flowers. The children saw the beauty of the flowers and longed to have them, "Sister Anguma, we want those beautiful flowers." She replied, "The tree is too big. We can't climb such a tree to collect flowers. It is not safe."

The children began to cry. They wanted the flowers by all means. Anguma began to feel bad for the children. She wanted to see them happy always. She climbed the tree and plucked the flowers. She dropped a flower to the children and said, "This flower is for mother." She dropped down another one and said, "This is for aunty." One by one she supplied flowers for all of them. The kids cheerfully picked them up and each one of them held them carefully in their hands always asking for more.

Suddenly she stopped. The children could not hear their sister's voice anymore, nor did any flowers come fluttering down. They looked up and saw that she was in pain and engaged in a struggle with the tree. The tree was swallowing her! Half of her body was already inside the trunk of the tree. Anguma looked at her younger ones and tears flowed from her eyes. The children cried, "Sister Anguma, come down. Please come down." But the tree swallowed her completely and she disappeared into its belly.

The children were frightened. They went back home without their sister. When their mother returned from the field, they clung to her and cried. "Why are you all crying?" she asked them. They were too scared to tell her what had happened to their sister. The mother thought the children were hungry and gave them food. But they refused to eat. Then she consoled them and asked what was wrong with them. They said to her, "Our sister was swallowed by a tree which she had climbed to get flowers for us."

Their mother did not want them to be unhappy. She replied, "Do not worry, children. Anguma will come back. Let us cut down the tree and get her out." She took out an axe and knife and went to the forest where the tree stood. It was a very big tree. She began to cut the tree with the axe.

A deer came along and asked, "Why are you cutting such a big tree?" The mother replied, "This tree has swallowed up my daughter. I want to get her back." Realizing that she was too weak to carry out the task she had set for herself she asked, "Could you, please, help me cut the tree down?" The deer agreed to help her. It took the axe and started chopping at the trunk.

The deer made a funny type of noise each time he swung the axe. The children were amused by this sound and burst out laughing. The deer did not like anyone laughing at him and said, "I cannot cut the tree!" and started to leave. The mother and children promised not to laugh again and requested the deer to continue with the job in hand.

The deer agreed and continued chopping away at the thick trunk. When the cut on the tree trunk was big enough, Anguma came out. She was very weak and still in a state of shock. They took her home and her mother gave her food. She ate only one grain the first time she was fed. She ate two grains the next day and increased her intake to three grains on the third day, etc. This went on till she could, finally, eat normally. Once she was able to have her normal meals, she recovered her health. Her mother was careful not to let her do much work or go out of the house.

Anguma had never gone to the dormitory (see 'Forward' page for reference) since the incident. Her friends missed her very much. They wanted her to come back and join them as soon as possible. But Aguma's mother wanted her to regain more strength. She fed her with good food and did not allow her to go out of the house or to work.

Her friends could not wait any longer. They said to her mother, "Please allow Anguma to come and sleep with us." The mother replied, "She is not strong enough. Moreover, you will make her sleep in the corner of the dormitory." The girls promised to keep Anguma in the middle of the hall when they would go to sleep. So, the mother felt she would be safe and sent her along with her friends.

As promised, Anguma slept in the middle of the hall. Her friends took good care of her. She woke up the next morning and went back home without any problem. This won the confidence of her mother. She was now sure her daughter would be fine enough to carry on with her normal activities once again. The next time she did not ask Anguma's friends to keep her in the middle of the room when they went to bed. They asked her to sleep in the innermost corner, just next to the wall. She slept peacefully and went back home the next day unharmed.

On the third day she was asked to sleep on the outer most side. Her friends also felt she was strong enough. The fear she had developed when the tree had swallowed her had gone off completely. Anguma did not make any fuss. She agreed to sleep in the outermost corner. But when everyone was asleep, a wild cat came and mauled her, pulling out her intestines and killing her.

There was something special about Anguma. The unknown forces had wanted her for something that no one knew of. No matter what her mother might have done to protect her, she was trapped in her own fate and had to do what the superior powers wanted of her. The gods always have it their way!

DITHUAILU
A multi-talented multi-skilled extraordinary girl

Many years ago, there lived a couple who had 3 beautiful daughters. One among them was Dithuailu. She was extremely clever and efficient in all kinds of work. Her mother thought there was something extraordinary about Dithuailu.

She would go fishing almost every day and return with lots of fish. However, this did not make her mother happy. Instead, she was worried. She tried to prevent her from going to the river. She would give her lots of work to do at home. Dithuailu would find ways to finish all her work and make time to go fishing. Her mother could never find fault with whatever chores she had been entrusted with.

One day her mother gave her a tin of till seeds and asked her to separate the white seeds from the black ones thinking she would not be able to complete this task. She thought she would not go fishing if she did not complete the work. But Dithuailu did it all.

It so happened that there lived a python in the river where Dithuailu used to go fishing. The python saw the beautiful girl who came daily to the river and he fell in love with her. He took the form of a man and visited her whenever she was weaving. He used to wear a black shawl when he came to the house. He would sit next to the girl and help her arrange the buns of wool and thread that were kept in her bamboo basket. The man never told her anything about himself.

Dithuailu wondered who the man was. She went to her mother and described everything that used to happen. She told her that she did not know where he lived, too, but when he left the house, she could see him go towards the South. Her mother thought it could be someone from the river because her daughter frequently went fishing and had never failed to bring fish whenever she went. So, she advised her to put Goh *(A ginger like medicinal root commonly used for many ailments)* in his basket the next time he visited. Dithuailu did as she was told.

Traditional weaving skills are appreciated even today

The next day, the man came to visit her. He complained of a headache and went away very soon. He reached home and had to go straight to bed as he felt quite ill. He requested his mother to bring Dithuailu to him. His mother transformed herself into a woman and went to get the girl. She informed Dithuailu that her lover was ill and that he wanted to meet her. Dithuailu was surprised. She told the woman, "How is that possible? I do not have any lover." The woman requested her to visit him even if he was not her love. She finally agreed and the two of them went down to the river, accompanied by a dog.

Zeilat, Tamenglong

On reaching the river bank, the woman asked her to go into the water. She refused to go in, afraid that she might get drowned. But the woman promised her that nothing untoward would happen. She suggested to her to send the dog in first in order to ensure her safety. The dog went in and came out after a while without even getting wet. Dithuailu was now convinced that she would be safe. She went into the water with the woman. Their house was on the river bed. When she went inside, she did not feel that she was under water. She found the man sleeping with the roots of the Goh plant on his head. Dithuailu removed the Goh plants from his head and he felt better. The mother was very grateful to her.

(Goh plant. The root is used to ward off evil and as medication)

To reward her she gave her a basket with some dry leaves and other waste stuff in it. She took the basket and went out of the water on to the bank of the river. When she tried to throw away the waste and dry leaves on her way back, there was thunder and lightning. So she took everything home and kept it as it was in the basket. Since that day, cattle in Dithuailu's family multiplied fast and they got rich harvests. Very soon they became prosperous.

One day she went to the river and did not return. People in the village went looking for her. They could not find her anywhere. They thought Dithuailu must have drowned. On searching carefully in the river, they found her body inside the python's nest. They pulled her out and took it home. Even many years after her death, she was frequently remembered among the Zeliangrong. Her incomparable skills and ability to do things quickly and efficiently are talked about among the people till this day.

REANG-DOI

An orphan becomes a hornbill

Long ago there lived a little boy with his mother and father in a village. They were a very happy family until the day his mother died. He was very young and still in need of a lot of motherly care and so his father married another lady. His stepmother turned out to be a cruel woman. She treated her stepson with hatred. She made him work very hard even though he was a small boy. She would be sad when she could not think of some hard work to allot to him. She did not like him to enjoy any leisure time at all. She would not allow him to play as the other children of his age did. Life was miserable for this boy who had lost his mother very early in life.

The young boy's father did nothing to stop the mother from being cruel to the boy. He loved his son but would fight back his tears in silence no matter what his wife did to her stepson. She treated her own children differently. She gave them good food and left them free to play all day. Her stepson had to eat whatever scraps she threw to him and babysit his step brothers and sisters. He would watch his siblings at play and think how fortunate they were.

One day, the stepmother could not think of any product-
ive work for him to do. She intentionally spilt grain on
the ground and mixed it with sand and dust. She gave
the young boy an empty tin and asked him to fill it with
clean grain. "I want this tin filled with grain by the evening," she said. "Just wait and see what I will do to you if
the work is not done before sunset."

The boy thought he had been given an impossible task
but, he was too afraid to tell her anything. He also knew
that his father would never speak up for him. He was sure
he would be beaten up if he did not complete the task.
He was truly frightened, so much so, he started to shiver.
Looking helplessly at the grain on the ground, he began
to cry, not knowing how even to start the task.

A bird sitting on a tree close by saw him cry and asked

him, "Why are you crying, my dear friend?" "My mother told me to pick up these grains from the sand and fill this tin," he replied. "I cannot finish this work in a day. So my mother will beat me." The bird took pity on him and said, "Do not worry, my friend. I am here to help you. We will finish the work today." That gave the boy a glimmer of hope.

The bird had sharp eyes and a quick beak. He picked up the grains real fast and the tin was soon filled to the brim. There was not a grain left lying about on the ground. The boy was relieved and thanked the bird for helping him and saving him from a thrashing.

From time to time his stepmother would ask the young boy to go to their field and chase away the birds preying there. The birds were his friends already. He did not have to chase any of them away. They kept clear of his fields and fed on the fields of the others. He was, therefore, glad to have this chore assigned to him as he would have no work to do and he could have some fun, though all by himself. Gradually he came to realize that he always had help coming to him when he needed it, though he never knew who his rescuer would be the next time.

As he grew older, he began to mingle with other young boys and girls in the community. There were two girls in the village who became close friends of his. They cared for this boy very much though they did not know of his troubles nor of his miserable life at home.

This boy and the two girls would go to work together in the fields. His stepmother never gave him good food for his lunch at the farm. He was ashamed to let his friends see the miserable food he had to eat. He did not want to eat with them. Whenever it was time for the meal, he would take his food pack and go to a piece of waste land nearby. He would have his meal quietly all by himself. Invariably he would find burnt rice or spoilt food in his packet. It was usually mixed with dirt and rat droppings. He would pick the food grains with the quill of a porcupine so as to avoid eating rat's dung.

A Porcupine

The young boy's friends were surprised at this strange behaviour of his – going off to eat his meal all alone! People who work together always eat together. They often asked him to have food with them and told him teasingly, "You want to have good food all by yourself." But he would just reply that he preferred having his meal alone.

One day his two friends decided to examine his food to

see what was wrong with him. They quietly opened the packet and found that his food was packed with burnt rice and droppings of rats. They felt very sorry for him. Till then they could not have even imagined what he was going through so very silently. They wanted to do whatever they could to help him. They threw his food away and replaced it with their own food. They then kept the packet back in his own basket.

When mealtime came, the boy took his packet and went to the place where he usually had food. He opened his packet and found clean and good food in it. He immediately closed the packet and went back to his friends. He told them, "Someone has mistakenly taken my packet of food." He gave it to them saying, "This is not mine."

The boy was worried that someone had mistakenly taken his original packet of food. He did not want either of his friends to eat the dirt and rubbish that was prepared for him by his stepmother. His friends told him, "No one has taken your packet. The one in your hand is yours." He was not convinced. He was ashamed and, at the same time, very sad. Seeing him so sad, his friends confessed to him what they had done. From that day on, he started having his food together with his friends. They gave him whatever support they could. Now that they knew something of his ugly secret, the boy started telling his two close friends how his stepmother treated him. There were days when he could not even bear the thought of going back home. He told them, "I am going to transform myself into a bird, a hornbill. I cannot bear my stepmother's ill treatment anymore." The two girls did not know how to console him. They could not come to terms with what he was talking about. "But I will return to meet both of you," he concluded.

He asked the girls to give him their sarong and shawl. They gave him 'Suihiak' (a sarong) and 'Mareipan' (a shawl) used by women. He used the Suihiak to cover his body and Mareipan shawl for his wings. For his beaks, he used the hard outer layer of a dried gourd.

(Suihiak is a traditional sarong used as a wrap-around by ladies. It is usually black in colour with red borders having artwork on it.

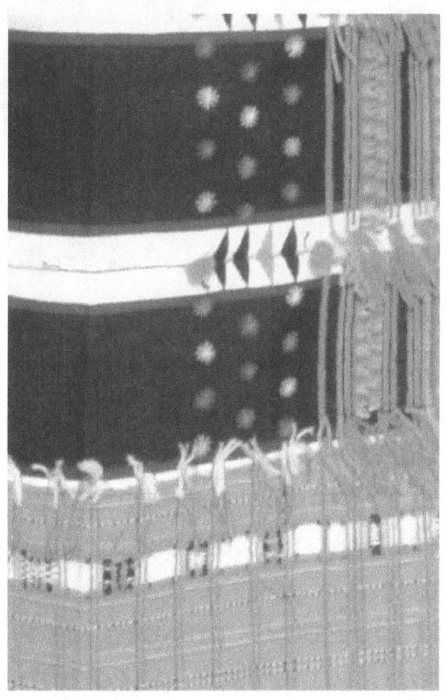

Mareipan is a shawl used by both men and women. Mareipan is also used by ladies as sarong and is also called Reang (hornbill) Sarong due to the close resemblance of its colour pattern to that of the hornbill.)

His two friends did not want him to go away; but he had made up his mind. He would attach his wings and feathers to his body, and practise flying every day. Gradually he extended the time and distance he could fly. When he felt he was proficient enough he told his friends that he was leaving them. As he flew up, the two girls shouted, "Come back, your wings are not proper." So, he came back and his friends mended his wings. When he took off a second time, they asked him to come back again saying that something was not looking nice.

This went on for a while. His friends were only looking for excuses to prevent him from abandoning them. He finally told his friends that he had to leave. He promised to come back at the main event of the harvest festival. He bade farewell to his friends and flew up. The two girls looked at him flying away and wept. They shouted, "Please, do not leave us! Come back!" But the boy knew he had to go. His life was miserable and there was no one to understand what he was going through. He flew higher and higher without turning back and was soon out of sight.

The Hornbill bird

A year later, the harvest season came. A certain man named Ahmang had harvested the largest amount of paddy among the villagers. He built a 'Tarangkai' (reference available in the introduction) to celebrate his achievement and feast on his harvest. On the day of the event, the girls were pounding paddy at Ahmang's house.

As promised, the hornbill appeared and flew above them. People noticed the bird and cheered, "Look! How beautiful the hornbill is!" The two girls also saw the bird and knew it was their friend. They waved and cheered, "How beautiful you are!" The hornbill took out two of its most beautiful feathers and dropped them. The feathers landed exactly on the tip of their pounding poles.

This made the girls proud of their friend. They continued to sing and pound the paddy. The stepmother of the boy came and saw the feathers of the hornbill. She felt jealous of them and wanted to have the feathers for her children, too. She said to the hornbill, "My son, you look so lovely. Can you send those beautiful feathers for your brothers, too?" The bird replied, "Mother, if you want the feathers, close your eyes and open your mouth as wide as you can."

His stepmother stepped out into the open and looked up. She closed her eyes and opened her mouth as wide as she could. The hornbill took out its feathers and dropped them down right into her throat. The feathers stuck in her throat and the stepmother was choked to death.

NIUMADUAN

Power vs Wisdom

◆ ◆ ◆

Part – 1
Background - The Creation of the Earth

In the beginning, there was nothing but water on the Earth. Only Melotiap, a supernatural being, lived there. As he was swimming one day, he came across an earthworm. He caught the worm and said, "I will eat you. You have been sent to me as my food." The worm pleaded with him not to eat it. Then Melotiap thought of using the worm to his advantage. He was tired of having to swim all the time and wanted to have some dry land he could take rest on. He said to the worm, "You must defecate as much mud as possible. Else, I am going to eat you." Fearing for its life, the worm agreed to do as ordered and produced lots of mud.

Melotiap spread the mud out evenly over the earth with his hands. He worked hard and made as much flat land as he could. The worm seemed to be enjoying his work and he kept up his production without a break. Finally, there was so much mud that Malotiap could not spread out all of it. The mud that was left untouched became mountains and hills. The mud that was spread evenly became the plains. Now there was a place for him to take his rest as well as for all the others who existed then. They could live now more comfortably without having to swim all the time.

The earthworm stretched itself out over the earth and at one point saw its own tail. It was not aware that the tail was its own. It tried to reach out and get hold of its tail but was unable to. It kept struggling to reach its tail, causing the earth to move. And that is how the earth started to rotate. The vigorous and persistent efforts of the worm resulted in something far bigger than what he himself had planned for.

Life evolved on Earth and it became more comfortable for them. With the passing of time, people began to have individual desires. One day Melotiap thought he would fulfill whatever people asked from him. He invited all the people on earth to come to him. Many people turned up and among them there were some who were jealous of him. He asked the people, "What would you like me to do for you?" One man replied, "I want you to bend down so that I can cook on your back." He actually wanted to kill Melotiap in this way.

Melotiap understood his true intentions. He could not refuse the man because he had promised to fulfil their wishes. He handed over some Ringpheang to his wife. (Ringpheang is something that has power to restore life to the dead). In case he died, his wife could use it to bring him back to life. He then let the man make a fire on his back. He did not survive the burns. His wife did as she had been told. When the cooking was over, she swept Melo-tiap's back with the Ringpheang and he was brought back to life.

He lived happily for many more years. After his death, no

one of his caliber and wisdom has ever again appeared on earth.

PART – II
Niumaduan – The wise man

Many years after the death of Melotiap, he was reincarnated as a man called Niumaduan. He was known to be a wise man who defeated power and wealth with his wisdom.

When it was time for Niumaduan to get married, he went to a nearby town looking for a wife. On his way, he met two beautiful girls. Seeing him, the two girls immediately made way for him. One moved to the right side of the road and the other moved to the left letting him pass between them. He could not find any suitable match for himself in that town. So, he decided to return home. On his way back he came across the two girls again. As on the previous occasion, one girl moved to the right side and the other moved to the left to give him way.

He noticed that they were the same two girls he had met on his way to the town but thought of it as a coincidence. On yet another occasion he happened to meet the two girls for the third time. They moved aside to let him pass in the same manner as they had done earlier. Niumaduan then thought it was God's way of sending him his life-partner. So, he chose as his wife the girl who always used to move to the right. She happened to be a very wise woman. It was said that half his wisdom was inspired by his wife.

One day Niumaduan and his father went together to

their field. They walked along for a while side by side in silence. He then said to his father, "Let us carry each other," and he kept walking. His father could not understand what his son meant. Starting out on their return journey, Niumaduan said, "Let's get an army for us." Later, when they had covered almost half the way, he said, "Father, let us climb on to a branch." His father could not understand anything of what his son spoke that day.

He went to Niumaduan's wife and complained about his son saying, "Your husband suggested many things to me today which he never had the intention of doing." Niumaduan's wife listened to her father-in-law carefully. She then explained to him the phrases used by Niumaduan in the following manner:
"Let's carry each other" - "let us talk as we walk along so that we don't feel the distance."
"Let's get an army for us" - "Let us get walking sticks."
"Let's climb on a branch" - "Let us cut down some branches to sit on them and relax."

After the explanation, she asked her father-in-law, "Did my husband talk to you while you walked along? Did he get walking sticks? Did he cut branches to sit on and relax?" He told her that his son had done all of that. She replied, "Your son has, indeed, done whatever he said!" and convinced her father-in-law with her wise answer.

PART – III
Niumaduan and the king

A certain powerful king also lived during Niumaduan's time. He and the king constantly competed with each

another. Both of them thought they were superior to the other. The king felt that he was the one in the higher position and he held real power over the people, while Niumaduan felt that his wisdom was superior to the power of the king or anything else.
Both of them wanted to prove their superiority in every way. They both agreed to perform several tasks from time to time to settle the matter of who was the superior of the two of them.

One day the king challenged Niumaduan, "Let us not bow down in front of each other. Whoever bows before the other is the inferior one." He thought that Niumaduan would not defeat him in this contest. He was sure that he would bow down before him at least out of fear or respect for the king.

To win this challenge, Niumaduan constructed a house with a slanting roof. At the front of the house the roof was high enough, but it narrowed down in the inside. Within the house he made a seat for himself. He rubbed the floor in front of his seat with elm so as to make the floor smooth and slippery. He then invited the king to his house. (*The elm tree produces slippery gel inside its bark. In the old days, Zeliangrong women used it as a hair conditioner due to its slippery and softening properties.*)

Elm plant

When he arrived, Niumaduan was sitting on his seat inside the house. He heard the king coming and said, "My king! My king! please, come inside." "Oh! A new house!" the king exclaimed and went in. The further he walked into the house, the lower the roof was. He had to bend down to reach where Niumaduan was sitting. When he moved closer, he slipped on the wet floor and fell down. He came finally to rest with his head just in front of Niumaduan's feet. So, the king had in fact bowed down in front of Niumaduan.

He said excitedly, "My king, you have bowed down before me." This made the king feel angry and embarrassed, but there was nothing he could do about it except to accept the fact. He had, indeed, fallen in front of Niumaduan as though he were bowing down to greet him.

The king thought he would give a fitting response to the embarrassment that was caused to him. He could not think of any idea better than the one of Niumaduan. He decided to try out the same trick that had been played on him. He built a house with a slanting roof and invited Niumaduan to visit him. Niumaduan knew the King's plan. He arrived at the king's place. The king invited him to come inside the house. However, Niumaduan did not bend forward but backward as he went inside. When he reached the king, he fell backwards with his head away from him. Then he said, "My king, I have not bowed down in front of you. I am undoubtedly the winner this time."

The king did not feel good about his defeat. He said to himself, "I will have to somehow defeat this man." He suggested another game and said, "Let us not obey each other. Whoever obeys the other is the loser."

Niumaduan agreed and thought of a plan. Early next morning, he climbed up the roof of his house. He sat on it and pretended to be repairing a leaking spot on the roof. As usual the King was taking a stroll around the village. He saw Niumaduan on the roof of his house and went over to see what he was doing. A rope then fell out of Niumaduan's hand. He said, "My king, could you, please, pass me the rope?" Out of normal courtesy, the king picked up the rope and passed it over to Niumaduan who was still on the roof of his house. "So, you have obeyed me!" he said to the King.

The king followed the same idea. When Niumaduan came to his house, he was constructing a house. Seeing him, the king dropped a hammer and pleaded, "Could you, please, pass me the hammer?" Niumaduan replied, "Please excuse me, I have a very urgent piece of work," and quickly went away. So this time too, the king did not succeed to defeat the wise man.

The king tried several other ways of proving his superiority over Niumaduan. Since he had lost two contests he looked for a task that no one would be able to perform. He told Niumaduan, "Bring me the village pond." Since it was the king's order Niumaduan could not disobey. "How can I win this time?" he thought. It was a difficult task. He was not sure if he could defeat the king with such an impossible task. The king said to himself, "This time, Niumaduan is sure to lose."

However, Niumaduan being a very wise man, had a brainwave as usual. He took hay and wove it into a rope. He laid out the rope from the pond up to some distance. At a particular spot on the rope he soaked it to half its thickness in oil. He burned off the half that was soaked in oil. He tied one end of the rope to a huge boulder inside the pond and stretched the rope out towards the village. He then sat back and waited for the king to make his move.

Since Niumaduan had not reported his progress, the king sent his soldiers to look for him. As soon as he saw them approach, Niumaduan caught the rope, pretending to be pulling on it. He told the soldiers, "Come quickly. Come and help me pull the rope. I am pulling the pond with this rope. It is tough, but it is getting closer. Come, help me!" The soldiers rushed towards him and caught the rope. When they pulled on it, it broke where it had been burnt. He said to the soldiers, "See, the pond has slipped back to its former position because you broke the rope."

The soldiers brought Niumaduan to the king. When asked for the pond he said, "My king, I was pulling the pond towards your house. But before I could reach your house, your soldiers came and broke the rope. So, it slipped back to where it used to be." The king could not believe what he said. "What nonsense are you talking about?" he shouted, and called his soldiers. He questioned them, "Did it really happen? Did you break the rope?" The king's soldiers nodded in affirmation. The king, hence was forced to accept defeat once again.

Since Niumaduan could accomplish the challenge placed before him, the king thought of yet another assignment for him. He said, "Catch a ghost from the jungle and bring it to me."

It was yet another impossible task. He went home and discussed with his wife how he could carry out this command of the king. Together they made a plan. He told his wife, "Boil a barrel of sugar solution and prepare a basket of cotton. Wait then till the king sends his man." She did as he had told her. Since Niumaduan did not turn up at the palace, the king sent one of his soldiers to inquire about him.

Cane Baskets used for storage

As instructed, when Niumaduan's wife saw the king's men approach, she came out screaming, "The ghost has come! A ghost is here!" Then she said to him, "Let us hide ourselves. I will show you where to hide," and she put him into the huge sugar bowl. His body was covered in sticky sugar syrup from head to toe. Pretending that she had made a mistake in the choice of the sugar bowl for a hiding place, she said, "Oh, no! Not here. Please stay over there!" and she pushed him into the basket of cotton.

The cotton got stuck all over his body and his face was all covered, too. Niumaduan was hiding somewhere while his wife played her part for him. He pulled the man out of the cotton basket and took him to the king. He said, "My king! I have brought you the ghost you asked for. Here he comes," and he pushed the man forward. The king was terrified and shouted, "Take the ghost away." The man replied, "My king! It is me, your servant." But the king was too terrified to listen or to understand and chased him out of his sight.

Even after repeated attempts, the king could not defeat Niumaduan. He knew that it was his wife who had been helping him with ideas. He wanted to marry her for her wisdom. So, his next plan was to kill her husband. He called Niumaduan and said, "Dig a hole in the ground to plant a pillar." His intention was to plant the pillar over him when he would still be inside the hole in the ground.

Niumaduan was in tension because he came to know of the king's plan. His wife saw his anxiety and asked him what was wrong. He told her what the king had asked him to do. "Take it easy," said his wife. She gave him the idea of digging another hole in their kitchen. When they had dug deep enough, they continued digging sideways till they had a tunnel that reached right up to the spot where the king wanted him to dig a hole.

Finally, Niumaduan started work on the assignment of the king. When the hole was deep enough, the king ordered his servants to plant the pillar with Niumaduan inside. However, he escaped through the tunnel he had made and came home.

The king was certain that Niumaduan was killed. He sent his soldiers to get Niumaduan's wife for him. When the soldiers came, they found him in the kitchen smoking. The news was reported to the king.

PART – IV
Exile of Niumaduan

The king felt hurt and humiliated because he could not defeat Niumaduan. He decided to send him away and fixed the day for him to go into exile. Since he was asked to leave after the day's meal, Niumaduan had an idea. He tried to delay his exile as much as possible. He told his wife not to cook in the kitchen. He set up a fire-place under the tree. He tied a pot to a branch and made fire under it in such a manner that the food would never get cooked. When the king's men came to inquire if he was ready to leave, he told them that he was still cooking. The king waited for some time and sent someone to inquire again. But he got the same reply. So, the king himself came to see Niumaduan and saw his style of cooking. "You are not trying to eat," he said, and asked him to leave immediately.

After Niumaduan left the kingdom, all the animals and birds stopped making any sound. The dogs stopped barking, birds stopped singing, cocks stopped crowing, and the cows looked as if they were never fed. The kingdom was absolutely quiet and silent.

The king realized that he was in a bad situation. He decided to call Niumaduan back to his kingdom. He told his soldiers to find him. They searched for him in all the villages in the vicinity of the kingdom and finally found him. When the news was reported to the king, he wanted to make sure that it was Niumaduan. He told his soldiers, "Take two cows of equal shape and size to him. If he can identify which is the mother and which is the calf, he is Niumaduan."

The soldiers took two cows of equal shape and size and

went to Niumaduan. He was sitting surrounded by bamboos and making ropes out of them. They greeted him and said, "We have come here for your help. We have a problem identifying which is the calf and which is its mother." Niumaduan said to them, "Put water in the basin. The mother will come first to drink, followed by the calf."

The soldiers reported this to the king. In order to be doubly certain that they had, indeed, found the right man, he told them, "Take to him a pole which has its two ends of equal shape and size. Ask him to identify which is the bottom and which is the top." Niumaduan was as usual making ropes out of bamboo when they came. "Could you, please, help us again in identifying the top and bottom of this pole?" they asked. He replied, "Throw the pole in the pond. The side that sinks is the bottom." The confirmation report went to the king. So, he said to them, "Bring him back to the kingdom. Tell him the king and all living things in the kingdom missed him."

So, the soldiers went and invited Niumaduan on behalf of the king to return to the kingdom. They took him on a horseback and rode towards home. The king wanted to reconfirm that the man was Niumaduan before he entered the kingdom. He stopped him on the way and said, "There is a bird in my hand. Can you tell me whether it is alive or dead?"

Niumaduan was not sure what to answer. If he said the bird was alive, the king may kill it and say it was a dead bird. He could not say it was dead because it could be a live one. He dismounted from his horse and asked the king, "Can you tell whether I will stand or run?" The king realized he could not challenge him in any way. He welcomed him back and gave him half of his kingdom to govern. He ruled over his kingdom wisely and justly for many years.

At times just being good, brave and strong does not solve problems nor save us from being defeated. Niumaduan teaches us to overcome challenges using our common sense.

THE FAIRY WHO MARRIED
A POOR BOY

◆ ◆ ◆

Long ago there was a boy who lived all by himself. Unlike other children of his age, he had to work hard to earn his living. There was no one to take care of him. He led a miserable life, hungry and lonely, with no one in the world to love or help him. His life was all about working hard just to make both ends meet.

The boy always felt lonely, abandoned and left out. He had to find some way to make his life more meaningful and enjoyable. Every moonlit night he would go to a pond which was a little away from his house. It was a lovely little pond. He would sit on a small rock under a tree and look at the beauty of the pond. The surface of the pond was enchantingly decked in beautiful lotus plants. The flowers glittered like silver in the moonlight and the sight of it would delight the boy.

This beautiful sight of the lotus and the cool breeze of the night gave him so much pleasure. It was always calm and fresh at night near the pond. Coming there gave him the only happiness in his life, a substitute for the companionship refused to him by the people around him. He went there as often as he could. It was his paradise, his home, his place of solace and repose. It helped him forget all his worries, at least for a while.

He came to the pond one evening after a day's hard work. Things were not quite normal that night. He saw that the lotus plants were damaged. Some were even crushed. The beauty and calmness of the pond were disturbed. Someone had entered the pond and swam about carelessly, destroying the plants and muddying up the water. The boy felt sad at the sight and he wept. His only source of happiness was ruthlessly damaged and almost gone.

He could not think of anyone who would come and destroy the plants deliberately to hurt him. There was no one who cared about him or took notice of his visits there. No one even knew that the lotus plants were very dear to him and that they were the only beautiful things he treasured. There was no reason at all for anyone to have a grudge against the pond and the lotus in it.

He wanted to know who could have inflicted such wanton cruelty on the plants. So, the next day he again went to the pond hoping to discover the identity of the destroyer of his dreamland. He sat there for a longer time, but not in his usual place. He hid himself behind a rock and waited to see who might turn up at the site.

He did not have to wait very long. He soon heard giggles and chatter approaching the pond. It was a group of young girls. When they reached the pond, they removed their gowns and let their hair down. They went into the water one after another. They were enjoying the cool and fresh water of the pond. They trod about and swam around carelessly engrossed in their own prattle and games. They were giggling all the time. They had nothing else in mind beyond their enjoyment of the moment.

They did not even notice that their carelessness was destroying the wonderful plants and harming the beauty of the entire pond. They were unwittingly destroying the only happiness of this lonely young man.

The boy was sad watching his beautiful plants being killed. He realized that these were not girls from his village. In fact, they were not girls or human beings at all. They were fairies. He quickly thought of a plan. He looked at the fairies and spotted the most beautiful one among them. In fact, she was the princess of the fairies. He managed to identify her gown, crawled up to it and took it away with him. He was extremely careful and no one saw him taking the clothes.

When it was time for them to return to their fairyland, they came out of the water and started dressing up. All of them picked up their gowns and started getting into them, that is, all of them except for the most beautiful fairy in the group. She searched for her dress everywhere but could not find it. She could not go back to fairyland naked, without her gown.

All the fairies helped her search for the gown, but they could not stay on when the final moment of the fairy hour approached. They returned to fairyland right at the last moment leaving the most beautiful among them behind, weeping for the loss of her gown.

The boy then came out of his hiding place and said to the fairy, "You are the one who destroyed my beautiful lotus plants. Now, as a punishment I will not return your gown." The fairy begged him, but he would not agree. He said to her, "The lotus plants were the only thing that gave me joy and you have destroyed them. You ought to suffer because of your cruel deeds."

The fairies, of course, had not intended anything cruel. They had merely been enjoying themselves. They had not noticed that their games were harming the plants. "How was I to know that someone liked these flowers so much, enjoyed looking at them and cared for them?" the beautiful fairy thought. However, she was sorry for her carelessness and begged for her dress. But the young man would not let her go.

Since the fairy was very beautiful, he decided to marry her. He said to her, "If you want your gown back you have to marry me." Having no other option, she married him. The boy, however, did not return the fairy dress to her so that she would never be able to leave him. He put it in a box and told her never to open it. He hid it away in the storeroom.

The boy lived happily for some time. He loved his wife very much and took good care of her. Not long after, the boy and the fairy got a child. He continued to work hard to feed himself, his wife and his child. It was the best time of his life because he had people he could love, care for and share his life with. But one thing never left his mind. He always feared that his wife would leave him if she ever found the gown.

One day, he was away for work as usual. His wife thought of a plan. She had not informed her parents that she had married and now had a son. She knew her parents would think that she was dead because she never returned from her swim in the pond. She wanted to meet her parents one last time to assure them that she was alive and fine. She would then return to her husband and son to remain with them forever.

She looked for her gown everywhere in the house but could not find it. Then she remembered the box that her husband had told her never to open. She went to the storeroom and opened the box. To her surprise, she found the gown. She decided to go immediately to meet her parents. She thought she would be back before her husband returned from work.

She left some food for her child and left the house. When she reached fairyland, she was met by her angry parents. They ordered the guards to close the gate so that she would not be able to return to her husband and child.

When the boy returned from the field, he found the baby all alone. He rushed to the store to look for the box where the fairy's gown had been kept. He opened the box and saw that the gown was gone. He felt very sad. He was afraid he would never find her again. His life went back to where it had begun. He was lonely once again. He had to work harder than ever before as he now had to look after his child too. He would get very tired after a full day's heavy work. In search of some solace, he returned to the only relaxation he used to have once - visiting the pond where he used to go earlier and where he had met his wife.

He would sit there for a long time thinking his wife might come once again for a swim with the other fairies. But she never turned up. Her parents had restricted her from stepping out of fairyland's gate. One day he got the flash of a bright idea. He plucked a lotus leaf and wrote a message on the leaf and asked the other fairies to pass it on to his wife. The next day, he got a reply from her. She told him what had happened. She told him the only way to get her back was by climbing up to fairy land. He could do this by getting on to the back of eleven white elephants standing one top of another in one heap. To achieve this, his elephants had to be young and strong.

White elephants are rare, and it took him many years to find young and strong white elephants. He managed to get only ten of them. By then he had grown old and knew he could not find anymore. So, he had to compromise with the criteria. He took one old elephant to take the number of his white elephants to eleven.

The elephants were made to stand one on top of the other. The ten young elephants stood strong and steady, but the eleventh, the old tusker, could not climb that high. Nor could it carry the weight of the others if it was placed at a lower level. So, he could not reach the fairyland to get his wife.

Since eleven young and strong white elephants were not found, the princess of the fairies could not come back and live with her husband and child. If only she had been able to return, it is possible that humans and fairies would be intermarrying and living together even today.

THE SUITABLE GROOM

◆ ◆ ◆

There was once a young boy born to a poor couple. He was the only son in the family. He was loving and obedient towards his parents. He was also helpful to people although he was from a poor family. There also lived at this same time a family of seven brothers. They were rich and powerful. The seven of them were united in whatever they did. They took care of each other well. However, they failed to look beyond themselves. Since they had never experienced scarcity of any sort in their own life, they were not sensitive to the needs of others. They did not feel the need to mix with people beyond their own family. Their style of life was in direct contrast to that of the young boy.

The young boy was helpful to people around him. One day as he was wandering about over the hills and valleys, he saw some clouds. They seemed to be confused as to where they ought to go. They approached the young boy for help. The boy told them, "Clouds are supposed to hover around in the atmosphere, just above the surface of the earth." The clouds were grateful to the boy for his piece of advice.

There was a king in the nearby kingdom who had a beautiful daughter. He was a kind and just man. When his daughter grew up and was mature enough, he wanted to find her a good groom. He was definitely looking for a man who had something more than mere physical strength and power. He wanted his daughter to be married to someone who was kind, wise and humble. It was not easy for him to come across a young man with the qualities he wanted. He thought of a plan to find the best person for his beloved daughter. He invited all the young men in and around the kingdom to compete for his daughter's hand.

Many young men came to the palace on the appointed day. The poor young boy was also among them. All the young men with power, strength, wealth, wisdom and good looks were there. There was no way the king could identify the best among them merely by looking at them. He decided to assign them some tasks to perform.

The first task was to bring a stone from a far-off place. The men were instructed to find a rock large enough to make a bathing place for the princess and bring it to her. They were taken to a spot quite far from the palace. The king's men said to them, "Young men, pick up the largest you can carry." The seven brothers looked at a large flat rock and said to one another, "What an easy task this is for us! Who can carry a bigger one than we can?" They lifted the boulder with no difficulty and set out towards the palace. The young boy also lifted a stone, but not as large as that of the seven brothers.

On their way back the seven brothers came across a bird. It was trapped in a bush and wanted to free itself. Seeing the brothers, it asked for help. The seven brothers did not even turn around to see who was calling out to them. They were concerned only about reaching the palace at the earliest.

The young boy also passed the same way. Seeing him, the bird asked him for help. The boy laid his stone down and freed the bird. The bird thanked him and said, "Someday, if you are in need of my help, I will be there." He picked up his stone once again and continued his journey. As they proceeded, the seven brothers met a snake. Some-one had placed a boulder over it making it impossible for it to move. Seeing the seven brothers coming, it asked for help. They did not even pause for a moment to look at it. They walked on. The snake was very sad, indeed.

When the young boy came along, it asked for help from him, too. The boy put his stone down and lifted the boul-der off the snake. The snake was grateful to him and said,

"Thank you my friend. Someday, if you need my help, I will be there."

The boy lifted his stone back on to his shoulders and continued to walk towards the palace. Seeing the boy struggling and lagging behind the seven brothers, the clouds came to his rescue. They lifted the stone above the boy and he could now move much faster. He had soon overtaken the seven brothers and reached the palace far ahead of them. He defeated them in carrying out the first task.

For the second task they were taken to another place and given a tin. The king's men spilt mustard seed on the grass and said to them, "Pick up only the mustard seed and fill your tin with it." The boy was stuck. He knew he could not fill the tin by picking the mustard seed all by himself. It made him feel sad and defeated. "I have lost the princess," he thought to himself. The bird he had helped happened to come by. It asked the boy why he was sad. On hearing the reason, the bird said, "Do not worry, my friend. How can I forget that you rescued me when I was in distress? In return for your help, I will pick up the mustard seeds and fill the tin." The bird started pecking at the mustard seed. With its sharp eyes and quick beak, the tin was soon filled. Happily, the boy took it to the king's men.

The final task was the most difficult. They were taken to the forest where they were set among thick and tall thorn bush. The king's men pointed towards a banana tree that stood in the middle of the thorns. They were instructed to collect the tenderest leaf from that banana tree without tearing it. This time, the boy knew he was going to fail. No one could think of a way to accomplish this task.

While he stood there numb, thinking he had lost the race, the snake came to his rescue. It slid into the bush and pulled out the tenderest leaves of the banana tree and brought them to him. The boy had outperformed all the rest, including the seven proud and selfish brothers. He had won in the accomplishment of all the tasks and earned the hand of the beautiful princess. The king gave his daughter to the boy and they lived happily ever after.

It was not the skills of the boy that helped him win the contest. It was his humility and genuine love for others that brought him success. Sometimes it is not enough to be capable and satisfied with themselves as those seven brothers were. We cannot call ourselves 'good human beings' if we are not sensitive towards the needs of others. When we think only of our own comforts and do not realize the need of people around us, we cannot truly be successful nor be happy.

ROKHEANG

Struggles of a stepson

In a village called Nkawluang near Tamei in Manipur (India) there lived a couple who had been blessed by God with a son by name of Rokheang. The boy grew up to be a very obedient and sweet child. His parents were very happy with his physical and mental progress and they enjoyed every moment of the time they spent together. However, their happiness was short-lived.

Rokheang's mother fell seriously ill and she passed away. It affected both the boy and his father very badly. They could not survive without a woman in the house to take care of them. His father had to work hard in the field. It was their only source of livelihood. There was no one to remain at home and take care of everything in the house, while his father worked in the farm. Rokheang was still too tender in age to take care of the household chores.

A Zeliangrong Naga village

In those days each family had to grow enough crops for itself. His father had to remarry so that he could get some help in the fields and at home. However, the new woman he married turned out to be a nightmare for Rokheang. The stepmother did not really like a child who was not her own. She treated young Rokheang with hatred. He could not play and have fun as other children of his age used to do. While the children in his neighborhood were out at their games, he was asked to do lots of work.

He would carry water, pound rice, go to the field and do all kinds of household work. However well he carried out all the tasks assigned to him, his stepmother had only complaints about him all the time. When he pounded rice, she would say that he had not done it properly. When he pounded well, she would say, he overdid it.

One day his stepmother gave him a container made of gourd and asked him to get water. "Make sure you do not break the container, else I will scratch your back with its broken pieces," she told Rokheang. He took the gourd and went to collect water.

(Gourd is a pumpkin-like plant. The skin of this fruit becomes very hard when it matures. It is mostly used as a container rather than as a vegetable.)

His stepmother had the deliberate intention of harassing the boy. She wet the floor of the entrance to the house and made it slippery by spreading the sap of the elm tree. When Rokheang returned, he slipped on the wet floor and fell, breaking the container to pieces. His stepmother screamed at him, "Did I not tell you to be careful?" She picked up a piece of broken gourd, and scratched Rokheang's back with it. Drops of blood flowed from the scratch wounds. But Rokheang did not fight back. He quietly went to the back side of his house and shed silent tears. It was painful, but he was too young and too scared even to let his stepmother see his tears.

The cruelty of his stepmother did not end there. She asked him to go to the field to deliver a packet of food to his father. She cut banana leaves from the garden and heated them for a few seconds so that the leaves became more pliable and resistant to tearing while packing the food. She prepared the packet, but made a small hole in it through which the gravy from the food could drip out. She then placed the package inside a basket.

She called Rokheang and said, "Take this basket to your father. He will be waiting for his meal in the field."

He obeyed his stepmother. Taking the basket on his back, he went to the field. Liquid from the food package began to drip and fall on his back. He could feel intense pain from the hot spicy sauce getting into the scratches on his back, but he continued walking towards the field. He cried out aloud knowing that neither his stepmother nor anyone else could hear him. He could not think of any other alternative but to bear whatever came his way.

When he reached the field, his father saw the tears in his eyes and asked him, "Son, what is wrong with you?" Rokheang narrated to him all that his stepmother had done to him. It made his father furious. He decided to teach her a lesson. He cut pieces of wood from a particular plant (Nsiang thing) for her to carry back home. The bark of this wood, when dried, contains particles that people are allergic to. The skin becomes very itchy.

One day, she came to the field. Rokheang's father took the pieces of wood, peeled off its bark, put them into her basket and told her to carry it home. Her skin had soon become so itchy that she could not carry it all the way back to the village. Fearing the anger of her husband, she ran off to her mother's house. She did not return for a long time until her husband asked her to.

Even after this incident, she continued to be cruel to her stepson. She would serve him his food separately. She never gave him any warm food. She would go to the extent of exchanging her warm food for some cold food from her neighbours to give to the boy.

Despite all the troubles he had faced, Rokheang grew up to be a handsome man. One day he went to the pond for a bath. On his way back, he saw a bird couple mating. They were so totally concentrated on what they were doing that he easily killed the birds and took their red feathers.

That day his stepmother could not find anyone among her neighbors who would exchange cold food with her. The neighbors had come to know about her treatment of her stepson. They decided not to exchange any cold food for a warm one. When Rokheang returned, she served him warm food. Rokheang was surprised to be served warm food that day. He did not know the reason behind the unusual change. When he had finished his meal, he took his flute ('alim' in Rongmei) and sat in front of his house. He played on it and sang a song, the meaning of which was,

> "My villagers, why is there no
> cold food for me today?
> I was served warm rice today
> for the first time in my life.
> What does it mean?"

Rokheang looked smart and well-groomed when he combed his hair and placed the feathers of the bird in the piercings of his earlobes. Wearing bird's feathers as ornament used to be common among men those days. It was a sign that the boy had grown to be a man. Red feathers are worn as earrings as they give a distinctive appearance. The hornbill's feathers were worn on the head.

His stepmother saw Rokheang and was startled at how handsome he looked. She felt attracted towards him and asked him to come inside the house. When he went in, she took his hands intimately and asked him to be her lover. However, Rokheang did not agree. In her frustration, she decided to destroy him. She ran out of the house screaming, "Help! Rokheang is molesting me!" He felt very embarrassed worrying what the neighbours would think of him, but kept silent again.

When his father heard of it, he tried to punish Rokheang by sending him away from the village. He did not know that his wife was the one who had tried to abuse him. It was only when she did not get what she wanted that she put the blame on him. Since his son did not say anything, he thought that Rokheang was at fault.

To carry out his plan of getting Rokheang out of the village, he asked him to build a raft. He did not tell him what the purpose of the raft was. He thought his son could not make a strong raft. He wanted it to break up when it would dash into large boulders under the strong currents in the river going through their village. His son would then die in the river.

Rokheang knew how to make a good, strong raft. He chose his bamboos carefully, tied the ropes very tight, and made a strong raft. When the work was done his father took him to the river. He put him on the raft and asked him to go away, wherever he wanted, but out of his village.

This was the worst part of his suffering. He felt betrayed by his own father. He did not know where to go from there. He sat on the raft and rowed slowly towards the other side of the river. When he reached the bank on the other side, he shouted, "Father, I did not do any wrong. It was my mother who took me by the hand and asked me to do what is wrong." Hearing this, his father asked him to forgive him and requested him to come back. But Rokheang was already hurt beyond healing as his own father did not trust him. He went away to a place called Luanjeang and settled there.

Not long after he settled in Luanjeang village (Near Tamei, in Tamenglong District of Manipur), he became very prosperous. After a few years he was able to build and own a Khangchiu (dormitory).

(The Khangchiu existed among most Naga tribes of North East India. It is a system where unmarried boys (khangchiu) and girls (Kailiu) come together for social purposes and spent the night together. There are separate dormitories for girls, boys and even for children in some places but, of course, in the same house and under the same owner. The owner of the dormitory is a respected person of the village with lots of power and prestige. It is usually the owner of the Khangchiu who provides all the requirements for the young boys and girls when they come together. A person once married cannot come back to the dormitory. The owner appoints a leader for each dormitory. In the old days, this system played a very important part in the education of the youth and the social life of the people. It was a matter of pride for any youngster to be associated with a dormitory.)

A (Khangchiu) dormitory for men in a Naga village

Rokheang's father and stepmother, instead, did not prosper after he left. They did not even harvest enough food grains to survive. So, one day his stepmother came to Luanjeang to borrow paddy. Hearing that the richest man in the village was Rokheang she came to him not knowing that he was her stepson. He recognized her and gave her many good things as gifts. She came back to him again from time to time. Whenever she came, he gave her plenty of food grains and would inquire after her husband. He would ask his helpers to pretend to wash and dry her clothes, and intentionally tear them. Then he would give her a new set of clothes. This made his stepmother very happy.

On her return home she would tell her husband about the generous man she had met. One day, Rokheang asked her to bring her husband along with her when she came to the village the next time. She went back home and told her husband about it. On her next visit the two of them made the trip together. When they arrived Rokheang gave them a grand feast with good food and wine. He narrated to them the story of his life and how he was ill-treated. They listened to him not knowing that he was talking about them. When he completed the story he told them who he was, and that the story was about them.

Rokheang's parents felt ashamed of themselves. His step-mother could not bear such acute embarrassment and died. His father tried to kill himself, too. But Rokheang stopped him. His father begged his forgiveness and took him back home where they lived happily ever after.

There is always victory of the good over evil no matter

how long it takes. This is seen in all the tales we read or hear. Our ancestors, too, were conscious of this ethics at whatever level of civilization they were in. It is debatable whether we, as individuals or as a community, are more ethical today than our forefathers used to be in their days.

DELIANGLIU

The goddess's send-off

Once there lived a goddess in a village. Her name was Deliangliu. Being a goddess, she was exceptionally beautiful. A wedding proposal came for her from another village. She accepted the proposal and prepared herself for the wedding.

Deliangliu wove clothes for herself and for the groom's family in preparation for the wedding. She collected all by herself the materials she needed. She acquired all the household items a new family would need, such as spades, baskets, utensils, etc.

A send-off party was held with all the young boys and girls of the village participating in it. They came together to bid farewell to the bride to be.

The next day, Deliangliu, her friends and her close relatives set out for the groom's village. Her parents were not among them. In those days it was believed that the bride's parents should not go along with their daughter if the marriage is to be held in some other village or town, away from their own community. So, Deliangliu's parents did not go along with her to the groom's village. The village was quite far away requiring them to halt one night en route. They had taken along with them all the tools and other house-hold items Deliangliu had collected for her new family.

When evening came, they looked for a suitable place to spend the night. They were close to a river; the water was good, and they decided to halt there. They laid down their baggage and collected stones to use as their pillows. It had been a long day for all of them. Tired from the day's walk, they soon fell fast asleep.

When morning came, only Deliangliu woke up. She looked around and could not see anyone alive. Instead, she saw that everything and everyone around her had been turned into stones; her friends, utensils, weaving sticks, baskets … all were turned into stones without losing their shape and size.

Deliangliu could not understand why it was so, but she could not wait to find out what was wrong or how to rescue her friends and relatives or her belongings. She had to reach her groom's house on time. She had to resume her journey. She got up and set out for the groom's house all alone.

Ever since it has been a part of the beliefs of the people that, when a marriage takes place outside their own village, the journey should be planned and arranged in such a manner that it is completed in just one day. No night halt is permitted on the way. The journey from the bride's village to that of the groom must be completed in a single day. The only reason why Deliangliu herself escaped being turned into a stone was that she was a goddess and not a mortal.

Perhaps this story was an expression of the desire of all parents that their children do not marry someone outside the tribe or even someone too far from their own home so that they could meet their children at least occasionally even after their marriage.

A NIGHT WITH A WITCH

◆ ◆ ◆

Once upon a time, there lived seven brothers. The eldest one went for hunting one day. He spent the entire day in the jungle hoping to get some animal. But he could not find any that day. On his way back, he came across an old woman living alone on a farm in the middle of the jungle. As it was getting late in the day, and having nowhere else to spend the night, he went to the old woman's house. He did not give a thought to any harm that might befall him by spending the night at the little cottage. The woman welcomed him very warmly and gave him good food to eat. She pretended to be very kind towards the boy and waited for the night to fall. She was excited to see a human there in the heart of the jungle and had plans for the night.

Night came and the boy went to sleep. The woman checked on the boy. Seeing the boy in deep slumber, she asked the termites to eat up the boy's bow and arrows. The termites climbed on to the bow and chewed at it. She then transformed herself into a witch and called out to the boy. He woke up and went to see what was happening. He saw the old woman, now turned into a witch and waiting for him.

A farm house away from the village

He ran back inside the house to get his bow and arrows. As he took aim at the woman and stretched the bow, it broke. The witch came laughing, pounced on him and ate him up.

His six brothers were waiting for their brother to come home with some animal from the jungle. They were eagerly waiting to have a great feast. He never returned. So, the second eldest boy went in search of him the next day. He went to the jungle and met the same old woman in the farm house. She welcomed him as she had done for his brother. When he went to sleep after food, she asked the termites to eat his bow and arrows, too. The boy could not kill the witch and he fell prey to her as well.

The third eldest among the brothers went next, then the fourth, fifth and the sixth, each in his turn. All of them met with the same fate. The youngest boy realized that something was wrong since none of his brothers returned from their hunting expeditions. He decided that he had to be extra careful and dared not take any chances. He took an iron bow and arrows and went to the jungle. As usual he met the old witch at the same place.

She welcomed him and invited him to stay in her house. He accepted the invitation and stayed with her. When night came and the boy was asleep, the witch asked the termites to destroy the boy's bow and arrows. The termites went to do her will but returned saying that their teeth hurt. The witch suspected something was unusual this time. The next day, the witch gave him food and blessed the boy. He then took his weapons and went to the jungle to hunt. The witch took on the form of a boar and came to attack him. The boy took out his bow and shot the boar to death, which is why the youngest boy of the family is always the rightful heir to the family.

The tradition is that the youngest son inherits the family's property and takes care of his parents and the rest of his kin. This is the practice to this day among the Zeliangrong Nagas.

TWO BEAUTIFUL SPINSTERS

◆ ◆ ◆

Once upon time, in a village of the Zeliangrong, there lived a large group of young boys and girls. Among them were two beautiful girls who were thick friends. They helped each other in every way and were always together no matter what activity they were engaged in. As was the tradition in those good old days, the young boys and girls of the village came together in their dormitories every night. (The practice was something like that of a club. The young members came together for social gatherings and then spent the night there. The closely knit social group helped the unmarried boys and girls to find their life partners among the members of the dormitory.)

As time passed each one of them found their partners, got settled and stopped coming to the dormitories. All the boys and girls of the age group of the two thick friends were married except for these two, the most beautiful girls of the village. No one had proposed marriage to them. In fact people avoided them no matter how nice they were to them.

The girls felt left out and sad. They began to wonder what was wrong. They could sense that something was not quite right with them. They felt embarrassed because no one made a marriage proposal to them.

One day they decided to find out the reason. They went to the owner of the dormitory and asked, "Master, we come to you for help. We are unable to find anyone to marry us. All our friends have found suitable partners. What is wrong with us?" The owner replied, "My dear girls, you have not done anything wrong." He knew exactly what was wrong with these two girls. But he could not tell them directly. He gave them a suggestion, "Take two straw pipes and put them between the two of you when you go to sleep. See what happens when you wake up."

(Some Zeliangrong communities used to believe in vampires. They could be recognized by their extraordinary beauty. Straw pipes, if kept under their pillow would turn to ashes. The bark of a peculiar tree called 'Ntoh thing', when placed under the pillow of a vampire could also reveal her identity.)

That night the two girls did as they had been told. The next morning they found that the straw had turned to ashes. "We are different. We do not have pure human blood. We are vampires. That is the reason no one has approached us for marriage," one of them said. They felt very embarrassed. They did not want anyone to know about it. "What shall we do now?" wondered one of them. The other suggested, "Let us go away from this village." They agreed on this plan of action, "No one wants us here. Let us not stay here any longer. We shall go far away where no one will ever find us."

The two girls did not even inform their parents. They headed towards the South and travelled until they found a suitable place to settle down. It was a quiet place where they could grow crops and vegetables. Since it was far away from their home village, they wouldn't meet anyone who knew them. Besides food grains, they also planted garlic on their farm. It grew very well. Their farm produced a rich harvest and they had all they needed or wanted. However, they missed their parents and friends very much, who did not even know where they had gone.

One day, they cut the garlic plants and tied them into two separate bundles so that they could send them to their parents. They tied a small knife along with the garlic leaves in each bundle. The bundles were sent to their village through some passersby. The mothers of the two girls received the garlic leaves and were happy to know that their daughters were alive. However, they did not understand why their daughters had left them. That made them sad but, at the same time, relieved to know that they were doing well. The garlic plants they sent were a sign that they were comfortable and had enough to eat and drink.

They opened the bundle and found the knives, too. With the knife, they cut the leaves into pieces. In the process, their fingers got cut. It was a small cut but, once the bleeding started, blood continued to pour out even after repeated efforts to stop the flow.

Since the bleeding did not stop, they consulted people who knew the traditional art of healing. No one could tell them what was wrong with their wound. They could not heal them. They went around trying out various remedies suggested by various practitioners. Finally, they found someone who could at least tell them what was wrong. He said, "The wound will not stop bleeding because it was caused by your daughters. Your daughters are hungry for blood. No amount of medicine will heal them."

The two mothers were shocked. "How can that be?" they thought. Then they began to recall that their daughters had left home without informing them. They had also wondered earlier why their daughters did not get marriage proposals despite being so beautiful. Now they began to believe that the man was right in his diagnosis.

They requested him for a solution to the problem. The man told them, "You have to kill an animal and offer it in sacrifice. While spreading its blood on a rock, chant the name of your daughters. Your fingers will then be healed." The women went back home and did exactly as they had been told. They brought slabs of rock and placed them in front of their houses. They killed a chicken and spread its blood over the rock. It did not take long for their fingers to heal completely.

The two girls continued to live by themselves away from the village. Vampires were not allowed to mingle with the normal villagers. They had to live in isolation although they were extraordinarily beautiful. In some very interior places, the practice still exists in some form or the other. (We have to wonder whether this ostracism, was in fact, born out of some people's envy of extraordinarily beautiful girls.)

GOD OF GODS
Raguang proves himself the strongest

A long time ago, there existed a god and a goddess named Changluaipu and Kamodiliu. One day goddess Kamodiliu went to bathe in the river. Changluaipu was roaming around in the hills and valleys. He passed by the river where the goddess was taking her dip. As soon as he saw her, he fell head over heels in love with her. He took the goddess with him and married her.

The goddess soon conceived and laid eight eggs. The eggs held eight gods within them: Raguang (God), Kougru, Buchaniu, Dui Ra (water god), Ieau Ra (god of farms), Roshi (god of evil), Mbahmei Ra (god of fools) and Dimai Ra (god of earth). Dimai Ra was the eldest among them. Mbahmei Ra was known to be brave and strong.

There was another god called Beanglaguang (king of earthquakes). He kept watch while the eggs were hatching. He was eager for these new gods to make their appearance. He thought of himself as extraordinarily strong and powerful. He wanted to challenge the rest of the gods and prove to them that he was the strongest of all and invincible. The gods in the eight eggs knew what awaited them and were afraid of hatching out. They peeped through the cracks in the eggshells waiting for a suitable moment to slip out. All of them were afraid of Beanglaguang, the king of earthquakes who, they thought, would kill them if they come out of their shell.

The eight gods held a conference to decide which of them would come out first. Dimai Ra (god of earth), the eldest among them said, "I do not have the strength to fight against Beanglaguang. I will be defeated easily. So, let me not hatch out first." All the others made excuses similar to what Dimai Ra had said. Mbahmei Ra (god of fools), the strongest among them said, "I can fight and defeat Beanglaguang; but I am not smart; I wouldn't know what to do next. So I shall not hatch out first." Since no one dared to come out first, they came to an agreement that whoever went first would be rewarded. He would be crowned the king of kings and god of gods but, of course, only if he defeated the mighty Beanglaguang.

Raguang was wise, mighty and powerful beyond description. He agreed to come out first. His strategy was to make an alliance with the enemy. Beanglaguang had a beautiful daughter. Her name was Modiliu. Raguang said to Beanglaguang, "If you really want us to come out, you must first give me your daughter in marriage. I will then give you a chance to prove your strength." Beanglaguang had to meet the demand of Raguang. So, he let his daughter Modiliu marry Raguang.

After the marriage, Raguang came out of its shell and fought with Beanglaguang. These two gods were well matched in strength. The fight went on and on for a long time. Raguang's wife stood by and watched the fight between her father and her husband. She was not sure whom to support. She said to herself, "My father has given me so much love. He has taken care of me since my birth. How can I see him getting defeated?"

Having said so, she looked towards her husband. A similar thought ran through her mind for her husband, too. She said to herself again, "I am married to Raguang now. I belong to him and have to share everything with him throughout the rest of my life. He will take over the responsibility of loving and taking care of me. What if he is defeated?"

Modiliu knew she had to make a wise choice because supporting either of the two combatants meant losing one of the two most important people in her life. She pulled out the longest hair from her head and approached the two gods at war. She tied it to Beanglaguang's legs. That made it difficult for him to maneuver. He fell down and was defeated by Raguang.

From then on, Raguang was declared the strongest God on earth. As agreed upon, he became the king of kings and God of gods. He came to be known as the wisest, mightiest and the most powerful of all. He was given the sole authority to rule the earth. Since then, he reigns and has power over everything and everyone else on Earth.

GUIREMANG AND GUILIANNEI

A story of undying love

◆ ◆ ◆

Buchaniu is a god of an ancient religion of the Zeli-angrong. This god is believed to have the power to incarnate himself in any form such as that of a tree, man, python or any other animal. It so happened that a long time ago, Buchaniu took the form of a man and met a woman named Kiuluanliu. He instantly fell in love with her and married her. They had a son and they called him Guiremang.

Guiremang grew up with his mother as any normal human child would. However, he never knew who his father was. He would hear his friends talk about their parents and siblings but no one, not even his mother, ever told him anything about his father. His friends would ask him where his father was and he never had an answer.

One day he asked his mother about his father. She told him he did have a father, but he would not be able to see him. This did not stop Guiremang from asking about him. He decided that he would see his father at any cost to avoid further embarrassment among his friends. Seeing that he was determined, his mother finally directed him to go to the river. She told him that he would have to go under the water if he wanted to see his father.

Guiremang did as his mother told him to. He went to the river and dived into the water. Deep under water he came across a gate. He told the gatekeeper that he had come to meet his father. The gatekeeper prevented him from going inside the gate immediately because his father had given him orders to that effect. However, Guiremang was very eager and he could not wait to meet his father whom he had been longing to see since years. He pushed his way in through the gate.

Immediately within the gate he saw two pythons, a male and a female. The male was his father. Trouble awaited Guiremang who had just fulfilled his wish of seeing his father. The python was furious on seeing his human son. He did not want him there when he was with his female python partner. He told Guiremang, "I am going to put you under a curse since you did not obey my instructions. I give you two choices. Your first option is to lead your life in oblivion and avoid all contact with fellow human beings. The second possibility for you is to live a life of fame but with lots of sufferings and, at the end of your life, die at someone's hand." The first choice meant that Guiremang would be struck with leprosy. He would have no contact with other human beings due to his disease and would be confined within the premises of his own home.

Guiremang thought he would rather be famous for something rather than spend the rest of his life hidden away in fear and shame. He therefore chose to live a famous life and die a violent death. His father told him his wish would be granted and he should take his leave immediately.

True to what his father had promised, he became well known. He spoke every human language and could even communicate with all other living beings. He was liked by all, women and men alike, for he was very charming. As he wandered along the Barak and Irang, he passed by a village occupied by the Khongsai tribe. As everywhere else, the women here too were attracted to him. He composed a song for them:

> "As I wander along the Barak and Irang,
>
> Beautiful are the women I see.
>
> With their necklaces like bands round their neck,
>
> Charming they are as my mother's clan.
>
> Long is their hair tied in a bun
>
> I extend my proposal of undying love."

He also composed a song in praise of women belonging to his mother's clan. (*As in many other cultures, when it comes to choosing women for marriage, the Zeliangrong also prefer women from mother's side*)

> "Women from my mother's clan,
>
> Wish I could make you mine.
>
> You are pure,
>
> Chosen and picked with care.
>
> Despise them not
>
> Hey woman! do not ignore and turn away,
>
> Let me make you my own"

Returning from his adventure among the Khongsai, he

wanted finally to settle down. No matter how popular he was, he did not have a feeling of belonging anywhere. He needed a place he could call his own. That is how he met a girl called Guiliannei. She was very beautiful. On hearing that Guiremang was looking for a place to settle down she asked him,

"How are the hills and the ponds?"

To which he replied,

"The hills and the ponds are as

good as the people of the land.

Oh, you who settled here first,

If you really are as good as the land,

We will follow you and live the same life."

Another man in the village by the name of Kouron was also in love with Guiliannei. Guiliannei, unfortunately, did not like Kouron. Like many other women of the village, she too loved Guiremang from the moment she met him. Kouron tried many ways to win her love, but never succeeded.

Guiremang was popular wherever he went. It was said that women were so infatuated with him that they even longed to own the things he had touched. They followed him wherever he went. However, this was not the case with Guiliannei's family. They did not like the love affair of their girl with Guiremang because he did not have a father. No one knew the truth about his father. They tried to get rid of Guiremang and break up their relationship.

In order to separate them, Guiliannei's father told Guiremang to find a bull that had a very peculiar type of horn. It was believed that bulls of this kind did not belong to any humans but to the gods. Guiremang was asked to bring the bull as a bride price for his daughter. Since Guiremeng could sense that it was almost impossible for him to find a bull of the sort the girl's father wanted, he thought he had to do something to save their relationship.

Before he left the village he took a bamboo basket and went to meet his love. Inside the basket was an earring. He said to her, "Keep this ring in the basket and keep a close watch on it. The earring will remain intact and closed if I am alive. The day the earring opens on its own, you will know that I am dead." Guiliannei did as she was told. She placed the earring carefully inside the basket and kept it hidden in her room. After Guiremang left she would check the ring almost every day. They had sworn a solemn oath that they would remain faithful to each other as long they remained alive.

It took Guiremang two years and more to find the bull. In the meantime, Kouron was desperate to get Guiliannei for himself and he hatched a plan. He told his aunt and sisters about his intensions. He asked them to go to Guiliannei and ask her to marry him saying, "Guiremang must already be dead. If he were alive, he would have returned by now." When the ladies went to Guiliannei and told her that her lover may not be alive any longer, she ran off to her room and opened the basket. When she found the earring intact, she came back and told them, "Guiremang is very much alive. I will not marry anyone else."

Many days passed. Guiremang did not return. Kouron's aunt and sisters came to Guiliannei a second time and said, "Guiremang is already dead, else he would have been back." Guiliannei ran off again to her room and opened the basket. She found the earring intact. So she told them, "Guiremang is very much alive. I will not marry anyone else." This went on and on repeatedly. Kouron and his family realized that Guiliannei had some means of finding out whether Guiremang was alive or dead. They kept a watch on her and, finally, found out that the secret was the earring in the little bamboo basket. They opened the basket when Guiliannei was not there and opened the earring. They wanted the girl to think that her lover was dead so that she would accept Kouron's proposal.

The next time when they came to ask for Guiliannei's hand, they repeated their usual formula. She ran towards her room to check on the ring. To her shock she found that it had opened. She was totally devastated. "No one else could have seen the ring. No one would deliberately do this. Guiremang must be really dead," she thought. Sad though she was, she did not see any reason to keep waiting for Guiremang. She agreed to the proposal of Kouron.

Guiremang in the meantime struggled to get the specified bull. He went far and wide in search of it. Since it was not an ordinary bull, he decided to try appeasing the gods and live among them as one of them. It took time to earn the confidence of the gods. Once he had won their trust through his faithfulness to them over a very long period of time, he was given the freedom to move around uncontrolled. Only then could he take one of the bulls of the gods and run away with it.

When he returned to the village after many years, Guiremang went with his bull directly to Guiliannei's house. He was sure that Guiliannei would be eagerly waiting for him. "The greatest challenge is over," he thought. But his expectations were shattered when he reached the house of his lover. He found that Guiliannei was married to someone else. It was the last thing he had expected to see after the long years of his struggle to get her. He had no other reason to stay on; he left the village with a heavy heart.

Since he no longer had a place where he belonged, he became a wanderer over the whole area. But wherever he went women would follow him. He knew the language of every village he went and bore the charm that men and women would fall for. He went to Serriam (Mizoram) where the queen too fell in love with him. This angered the king and he beheaded Guiremang.

True to what his father had told him, Guiremang did not have a happy life. He did not get the love of his life after having gone through so much trouble only for her. He had to bear all the sufferings that came to him as a result of the curse placed on him by his father. He was killed by his opponents who were jealous of him. Though beheaded, he died a slow death bearing the pain of his wounds and a broken heart.

Even in anguish he could not let go of the memory of the woman he loved. Before he breathed his last, he sang a song expressing his love for Guiliannei and his wish that she had responded to his proposal. His eyes were filled with tears. Seeing his anguish and his weeping eyes, a woman wiped them dry letting him continue his song till death relieved him of his pains. Here goes the song:

"By a roadside that wound up a hill

Guiliannei stood like the queen of the hills

I called out to her in admiration.

But response I got none.

Oh what Love! What a Love!

With a bracelet on her wrist,

she stood lost in thought

My youth gone waste admiring this bloom

This flower that is so short-lived."

As in all other societies, obedience and respecting the wishes of elders in the family are held as virtues among the Zeliangrong. Even today, parents in very traditional families narrate the story of Guiremang when their children go against their wishes.

THE SEVEN SONS

◆ ◆ ◆

A couple had seven sons. They worked on their farm for their living. One day all of them went out to start the process for the new cultivation. Clearing and burning of the jungle are usually done in the winter season. Once the trees and bamboos are cut down and burnt, the ground is prepared so that seeds can be sown just before spring.

The seven brothers took a knife each and went to the forest. Their father also went along; but he had forgotten to take his knife. They cut a piece from a bamboo and sharpened its edges so that it could be used as a knife. They gave this bamboo knife to their father.

This family had a peculiar tradition. Before they commenced any task they would make some agreement on one or another aspect of their work. That day they agreed that the one who put in the weakest performance would be placed on the tiger's path as his punishment.

Since their father used a bamboo as a substitute for his knife, he could not progress much in his work. When evening approached, they came together to see who was the weakest performer. It was their father who could not do much work because of the tool he used. The eldest son expressed his opinion to the rest of the brothers, "We have no option but to put our father on the tiger's path.

We cannot break the agreement." The rest of the brothers nodded their consent except for the youngest son. He did not like the cruel idea of his brothers.

As there was no one else to support the youngest son's point of view, their father was put on the tiger's path. They left him there and went home. A tiger came by and ate him up. The next day, the sons went to the jungle to look for their father. They found that the tiger had taken his life. Although they had placed him in such serious danger, they had not actually expected a tiger to come that night and eat him up. It was meant to be just a punishment to teach the laggard to work harder. By the bad luck of their father, it had turned out to be far too cruel and had cost him his life. This made them very angry. They made up a plan to take revenge on the tiger.

The eldest boy picked up his bow and arrows and went looking for the tiger. On his way he met a wild cat. It was making a pounding basin on a log of wood. The cat asked him, "Where are you going, my friend?" "I am going to take revenge for my father's death," he replied. The cat wanted to check whether the boy was capable of killing the tiger and said, "My dear friend, try shooting this pounding bowl with your bow and arrow." The boy took out his arrow and took aim. He hit the basin but could not break it. The wild cat said to him, "Go back home, my friend. Do not risk your life." The boy refused to heed this advice and decided to go on.

As he proceeded on his journey, he met an elderly woman. She asked him, "Where are you going, my son?" "I am going to take revenge for my father's death," he replied. She asked him to shoot the pigs she was feeding.

The boy took out his bow and an arrow, and took aim. His shot missed the pigs. Seeing his performance, the woman tried to stop him from meeting the tiger.

The boy was adamant. He did not want to return home and be embarrassed in front of his brothers. He went ahead to meet the tiger. Right in the middle of the woods he came across a house. An old witch lived there, sharing her house with the tiger. She greeted him and asked him, "Why are you here, my son?" The boy answered, "I am here to hunt animals." She invited him to stay in her house. When evening came, she fed him with good food and told him to go to bed early. After sometime, she checked whether the boy was asleep. Finding the boy in deep slumber she said to the termites, "Eat up the boy's bow and arrows." They munched away at these weapons till next morning.

After a while, the cock crowed, and the witch fed the chickens. She asked the tiger to come out of the house. The boy saw the tiger and took out his bow and arrows. The tiger roared and charged towards him. As he stretched his bow, it broke because the termites had eaten away a good part of it. The tiger pounced on him and ate him up.

The six bothers were waiting for their eldest brother's return. When he did not show up the second son went looking for him. He met the wild cat and the woman. When he could not accomplish the task of shooting the pounding bowl nor the pigs, he was also asked not to go on. But he went ahead just as his elder brother had done. He met the same fate at the witch's house which sheltered also the tiger. Since he did not return, the third son went looking for them; then the fourth, fifth, and sixth made their attempts and met the same fate.

The youngest boy was now the only one left. He told his mother that he would go to avenge his father and brothers. Since none of those who had gone on the same mission ever returned from their trip, his mother tried to stop him. She was afraid that he would also get killed as his brothers had been.

The boy was resolute and determined. Seeing that he had made up his mind and could not be dissuaded, his mother blessed him and gave him a bow and some arrows made of iron. He took these and set out on his journey. Just as his brothers had done, he met the wild cat who was making a paddy pounding basin. When the boy came, the cat asked him to shoot the bowl he was making. The boy took careful aim and shot it, splitting it into two halves. "Well done, my boy!" the cat said and wished him good luck.

The boy also met the elderly woman who was feeding her pigs. She asked him to shoot one of them. The boy took a correct aim and killed a pig with a single arrow. "You are lucky, my son. Stay over for the night," she said, and gave him good food so that he could rest well. The next morning she blessed him and let him go.

When he reached the tiger's house, the old witch was there. She greeted the boy and asked, "Why are you here, my boy?" He replied, "I came here to hunt animals." She invited him to stay for the night. When the boy was asleep in the night, she asked the termites to eat his bow and arrows. The termites returned after some time complaining of pain in their teeth. "There is something wrong," she thought.

The next morning the cock crowed. "Grandfather dies....son lives," the cock sang. "What is the matter?" the tiger thought. It did not want to risk its life. So, when the witch asked him to come out, he refused to do so.

The boy was well armed with his good bow and arrows and waited for the tiger. "Come on, come out," he challenged the tiger. "You are the one who killed my father and brothers. Now come and eat me, if you dare," he shouted. The tiger was provoked at these daring words from such a young boy. It came out roaring and charged at him. He took a good aim and shot at its head killing it with a single shot. He chopped off the tiger's head and went home to his mother and lived with her happily ever after.

'Bravery' and 'revenge' were considered virtues in the past as much as bravery is today. Instead, 'revenge' is perceived now-a-days as barbaric and primitive depending on the way it is achieved.

SELFISH MOTHER

◆ ◆ ◆

Once upon a time there lived a mother and two children in a small village. The elder one was a boy and the younger one a girl. They were very poor. Their mother worked hard to make both ends meet.

A famine broke out in that village. Their farms failed to produce enough food grains. People in that village started looking for alternatives in the neighboring villages. Some people would borrow food, whereas others exchanged whatever they had for food grains.

The mother and her two children also had nothing to eat. "My dear children, I will go to nearby villages in search of food for us. In the mean time, the two of you will have to manage with whatever we have here," She said. She left behind some stock of food for her children. She told them, "I will be back soon. Do not go looking for me even if I am late in returning." She then left. She went to the neighbouring villages but could not find any food grains. She kept going from one village to another, each time farther and farther from her home. Finally, she came across a rich man in one village.

The rich man had many cattle and lots of food grains. He lived with his younger sister. She entered the house and told them why she had come. The rich man was kind and generous. Knowing that the man was rich, the mother of the two children did not want to return home. She asked the man to marry her. She did not tell him about the two children she had left behind.

The two children waited for their mother's return. The food stock that their mother had left behind got over. They did not know what to do. They decided to go looking for their mother. They went to the nearby villages and asked people about their mother. No one would give them any useful information about her. They would, instead, say, "We don't know anything about your selfish mother."

This made the children sad. They moved on from one village to the next. Finally, they came across a kind lady. She took pity on them and gave them something to eat and then told them where they could find their mother. She pointed out a village to them and said, "Look that side. Your mother's house will be on the side of the road. The compound wall is made of dry cow dung. As you enter the gate, there will be a shed where they pound paddy. Your mother will be in that house."

She gave them some more food and let them go. The two children went looking for the house whose compound wall was made of cow dung. Finally, they found the place and they were very excited, indeed! They stood at the gate and called out, "Mother! Mother!" But there was no response. They made sure that it was the correct house. They called out again, "Mother! Mother!" A woman's voice replied from inside the house, "I have no children. How can I be your mother?" Hearing her say that, her husband said to her, "Call them inside even if you don't have children."

So, the children were called inside. Their mother was not happy to see them in her new home. She told them, "I told you I have no children. If you still feel that you are my children, you will have to prove it yourselves." She took a pounding shaft and planted it very deep and tight into the ground. Then, she said to them, "Whoever can pull this shaft out will be accepted as my child." Turning to the boy she said, "Come and pull this out." The boy tried to pull out the pounding shaft. He pushed and pulled the shaft trying to loosen it. But he did not succeed. Then, the girl tried the same and since it was already loosened a little through the efforts of her brother, she managed to pull it out.

Since the boy had not succeeded, their mother said to him, "You are not my child. Go home and take care of yourself." To the girl she said, "I will keep you in this house so that you can be my babysitter."

Since he could not prove himself, the son had to leave the next day. The kind man's sister packed some food for him to eat on the way. He took the package and set out on his journey. On the way, he went to attend to nature's call. He left his food package behind on the roadside. A crow saw it and ate up all the food. The boy came back and saw that his food was all gone. He did not know what to do. He thought of his mother, but he was not sure she would be happy to see him again. Knowing that he had a long journey ahead of him, he could not proceed without having something to eat on the way. He went back to the house where his mother and sister were.

The kind man's sister received him and asked, "What is wrong, my boy?" He narrated to her what had happened. Then she said to him, "Don't worry, my boy. I will pack food for you again so that you can reach home." She gave him a fresh packet of food before he left the next day. The same thing happened to him again when he went to attend to nature's call. He had no choice but return to the house once more.

The kind man's sister knew what was happening. He called the boy and said, "Next time when you go to attend to the call of nature, set a trap for the crow just near the food package. When caught, ask the crow for its necklace. Threaten to kill it if it refuses. Take it home with you. It will bring you good luck."

The boy listened to her carefully and set off on his journey again. On the way, he set a trap near his food package and hid in the jungle. Thinking that the boy was gone, the crow came to eat the food. It got caught in the trap. The boy came out of the bush and caught the crow.

He said, "Now I got you. You were the one who ate up my food yesterday and the day before. I will kill you because you caused me a lot of trouble." The crow replied, "Please, do not kill me. If you let me go I will never do it again." "How do I know you will never repeat what you have done? I have no option but to kill you," said the boy.

The crow replied, "You can kill me if I repeat my crime. Please, let me go now." The boy looked at the necklace it wore and said, "If you do not want me to kill you, give me your necklace." The crow refused to give it to him. The boy caught hold of its neck very tight and said, "Give it to me or you will die right now." Fearing for its life, the crow gave the boy its necklace.

As directed by the rich man's sister, the boy took the necklace home. He did not do anything until he got home. He took out the necklace and asked it for whatever he wanted. "A house!" he said, whipping the necklace at the same time. A house materialised in front of him. He then asked for cattle, food grains, servants, etc. He got whatever he asked for. He asked for a beautiful wife, too, and he lived like a prince with her thereafter. He heard of his mother only when famine broke out again and her family did not have enough to survive. She came asking for food grains not knowing that it was her own son's house.

He received her and treated her well. In the evening, he asked his servants to prepare a good dinner too. After dinner, he said to his mother, "Let me tell you a story." He began narrating his own story. He described how he and his sister was abandoned by their mother when famine broke out. Hearing the boy's story, the mother exclaimed, "Oh my goodness! What kind of a mother she must be to abandon her own kids?" The boy continued narrating his story.

When he was finished, he revealed to her everything and pointed out that the mother he was referring to was her. She felt very ashamed and asked for his forgiveness. But he told her, "I will give you whatever you need. But I cannot forgive a mother who denied her son when he needed her most." Hearing this, his mother could not face the embarrassment. Something exploded in her head and she

did not survive it to meet again her husband and children, whom she had abandoned a second time in her life.

A WORTHY PRINCE

◆ ◆ ◆

A king had eight sons. They lived in harmony among themselves. The king took good care of them and they had all they wanted. The negative consequence was that they remained too dependent on their father. None of the sons seemed suitable to take over the throne as a responsible king.

As the king grew older and older, he began to think who the right person could be to reign after him. He wanted his successor to be brave and strong. He was worried because none of his sons was capable enough. He thought of a plan to choose the best among them. One day he said to them, "My dear sons, you are all grown up now. I have a task for all of you. Can you fulfil my wish?" All of them replied, "Yes father, tell us what you want us to do."

He pointed at a hen that was sitting on a banyan tree. The hen was not of an ordinary species. It was a hen that laid eggs of gold. "Look at the hen on the tree. Its eggs are of pure gold," he said. He asked his sons to climb the tree and catch the golden hen. All of them were scared, except the youngest who said he would do it. As he climbed up the tree, the hen fell to the ground. There was a crack in the earth just below the banyan tree. The hen fell right into this crack.

All of them were afraid even to go and look down the crack. The youngest son took the initiative again. He went down into the crack and caught hold of the hen. Once he had it in his hands, he could not climb back up to the surface all by himself. He asked his elder brothers to drop a rope down the crack so that he could hold it and climb back up.

The elder brothers did drop a rope for him. But then an evil thought came into their minds. They did not like the idea of the youngest among them doing what they could not do. If he managed to climb back up with the golden hen, their father might think that only he was courageous. He would be favored for fulfilling their father's wish.

As he was making his way up, his brothers looked at him and were filled with envy. They asked him as though teasing him, "Should we now cut the rope?" He answered them in an equally jovial manner, without even considering what he said, "You may do so, if you wish!" The elder brothers took advantage of what he had said and cut the rope.

The boy fell back down into the crack in the earth. He fell so deep down inside that he came to the land of imps. He lay there stunned, unaware of where he was and what he was doing. One imp saw him and took him to her house. She nursed him and got him well, and eventually took him as her husband.

He lived there for many years. Many children were born to him and his imp wife. He and his wife would gather food for their children and spend time with them. He had become very much a part of their lives. He had grown very close to them, too, as if they were his human companions.

One day, his children were playing a game called "Goh toumei". As he stood and watched them play, one goh rolled towards him and came to a stop just beside his toe. He stamped on it quickly so that no one could see that it was under his foot.

(Goh is the seed of a type of tree. It is flat and round. When it is dry it becomes very hard and black. The game is played between 2 opposing persons or 2 opposing teams. Each player has a seed. The seeds of one team are made to stand on the ground in a line. The members of the opposing team roll their seeds towards the standing ones, to touch them and make them fall. There is a variety of steps they could take before they set their seeds rolling. The team that clears the greatest number of steps is the winner.)

The children came running looking for their toy, but could not find it. He quietly took the nut and went far away so that no one could see him. He then threw the nut on the ground and said, "If I am to meet my parents and siblings again, let this nut grow into a tree that touches the sky." Not many days after, the nut began to grow. It became taller and taller till it really seemed to touch the sky.

When the plant was big enough, he decided to go back to his parents and brothers. But whenever he climbed up the tree, his children would cry out and say, "Father, please come back." He could not ignore the cries of his children. He had lived long enough to love and care for them as though they were fellow human beings. He had forgotten that they were different. His father's heart would not let him leave when he heard his children crying out to him to return. He made several attempts, but each of them ended in the same way. One day he decided to go on up the tree no matter how much his children begged him to return.

He took the golden hen and climbed up the tree. As usual his children began asking him to come back. He looked down at them for the last time and thought for a while. He knew that if he went down again, he would never climb back to this world. The thought of going away from his children made him sad. Tears rolled down his face and fell on his children. They cried out, "It is raining! It is raining!" and ran towards their mother.

Hearing the children calling out in this way to their mother he remembered once again that he was in a different world that did not belong to human beings. He decided not to look back again. He held the golden hen tightly and climbed up the tree till he reached the surface of the earth. He went straight home and gave the golden hen to his father. His father was happy with him and wanted to share his power and wealth with him. He was angry with his elder sons for ill-treating his youngest.

As a reward for what he had done, the king asked this youngest son to make a choice of two options: first, if he wished, the kingdom could be divided into two. One part would be governed by him and the other by his son. The second option was to take full charge of his elder brothers and he could do with them whatever he wanted to.

He preferred to choose the second option as it gave him the possibility to take revenge on his brothers. He was furious at them for their treatment towards him. He made one brother blind, another lame, a third dumb, a fourth deaf, etc. He then used them as slaves to take care of his house. Thereafter, he lived in prosperity with his father.

KEANGCHEIPU
Cleverness under fire

Keangcheipu was a clever man. One day he went to the forest to cut bamboos. He met a tiger on the way. Keangcheipu looked like stuff for a good, tasty meal. It wanted to know the route he would take on his way back from the woods to the village. It asked him, "Keangcheipu, which way are you planning to return?" He answered, "I will be returning by the footpath over those hills." The tiger did not want to miss its chance of killing the man. It sat on the path through the hills and waited for his return. However, Keangcheipu did not come that way. He had understood the intentions of the tiger. He had taken the way through the valley. This route through the plains was longer, but he could avoid the danger posed by the tiger.

The tiger's plan failed. Not long after, Keangcheipu came to the forest again to collect bamboos. The tiger met him a second time and asked, "Keangcheipu, which way are you planning to return?" He answered, "I will be returning by the way through the plains." The tiger waited for him in the valley, but the man took the hill route. The tiger's plan had failed again.

The third time he met the tiger, the same thing happened. Therefore, at the fourth encounter the tiger waited for Keangcheipu in the hills because he had said that he would be returning by the plains. The tiger was certain that he would this time finally get its chance to eat him.

Towards evening, Keangcheipu returned by the footpath through the hills. He was carrying with him lots of bamboos and strips of cane. The tiger was happy to see him. It knew its plan had worked this time. It did not, however, know why he was carrying ropes and bamboos. "Why do you carry so many bamboos and ropes?" it asked. Keangcheipu did not take time to reply. "They are for making a cage for my wife and children so that I can tie them high up in a tree when strong winds come," he said. "They will thus be safe in any storm." The tiger thought it was a good idea and requested him to make one also for itself.

There could not be a better opportunity to tie the tiger up. Keangcheipu at once took out the bamboos and ropes and started making a cage. In the mean time, he asked the tiger to locate a tree with a very strong trunk. The tiger went around striking the trees one by one to check whether they were strong or would break easily. The trees toppled over because the tiger's blows were really very hard. Finally it struck at one tree that did not break. Keangcheipu told him that it would be strong enough to take the weight. He then put the tiger in the cage, closed it and pulled it up to the top of this strong tree so that it could not escape. He wanted the tiger to suffer and die because it had made several attempts to kill him.

He then shouted to all the animals, "Whoever has anything against the tiger may come and take their revenge. He is tied up here." All the animals feared the tiger. Although they had frequently been angry with it, they had not been able till then to do anything because the tiger was stronger than most of them. Hearing Keangcheipu, many animals turned up. Some of them slapped the tiger and others spat on it. There were yet others who did not even dare to come near it and went away.

The tiger was desperate to free itself. It was waiting for someone to come to its rescue. Whenever it asked for help, the animals would flee because they were afraid. A deer passed by. The tiger said to the deer, "Could you, please, help me come out of this trap?" The deer replied, "No way. You will eat me if I help you." The tiger promised not to do that. The deer picked up courage to go to the cage. When it cut one rope, the tiger opened its mouth and roared. The deer was terrified and ran away.

Next a bear came along. "Could you, please, help me come out of this trap?" asked the tiger. The bear also replied that it would not help the tiger because it would be eaten up. The tiger promised not to do that. So the bear went and cut another rope from the cage. The tiger opened its mouth and roared once again, terrifying the bear. So, the bear also went away.

Finally it requested a wild cat to open the cage and set it free. The wild cat cut the rope with its teeth and the tiger was set free. As soon as it came out, it tried to kill the wild cat. The cat ran for its life with the tiger in hot pursuit. The cat escaped into a rabbit's hole and hid in it. The tiger sat at the opening to the hole waiting for the wild cat to come out.

Then a wild boar came along and saw the tiger. It asked the tiger, "My dear friend, what are you doing here?" The tiger replied, "I am waiting for my food. Why don't you join me? Come and dig the rabbit's hole. We shall share the food." The boar agreed and started digging the rabbit's hole.

The boar found the wild cat and killed it. It did not tell the tiger that he had succeeded. It started eating the meat by itself. The tiger saw the boar chewing something and asked, "My dear friend, what are you chewing?" The boar pulled out some roots from the earth and said, "I am only trying to remove the roots of plants. They are blocking the hole." The tiger believed him and did not say anything. After a while it saw the boar chewing something again and asked, "My dear friend, what are you chewing?" The boar pulled out some more roots and said,

"There still are some roots blocking the hole. I am chewing them out."

The tiger could not believe the boar anymore. It was obviously not chewing on the roots of plants. The boar was eating the wild cat all by himself. That made the tiger furious because it was very hungry. So, it wanted to fight with the boar. The tiger challenged the boar to an open duel. They agreed that they would hold their fight seven days later.

Both of them made preparations for the great contest. The boar rolled itself in mud every day. The layer of mud had become thick enough by the seventh day so that the tiger would not be able to bite him easily. The tiger dressed itself up in leaves and came to face the boar. The tiger was given the first chance to attack. It charged towards the boar and tried to bite its back; but only the mud came out. The boar did not get hurt. When the turn came for the boar, it ran towards the tiger and bit it hard. Blood oozed out and the tiger died. The boar became very proud of its victory. It went around biting the trunks of trees and plants to show off its strength. In the process, its teeth got stuck in the stem of a banana plant and he, too, died.

The animals in the forest ate the dead body of both the tiger and the boar. They gobbled the meat down greedily and would not stop even after they were over-full. Finally, they also lay dead at the same spot, killed by their greed and over-eating. The bodies of the animals rotted and only their bones were left behind.

A rabbit passed by one day. He saw the bones of the animals on the roadside. He picked up one and blew on it. It made a sound. Then he picked up another bone and blew on it, too. It also made a strange hollow sound. He kept picking up bones and blowing on them one after another. As he kept checking the bones out, he happened to blow on one particular piece that produced a very sweet sound. He noticed the difference immediately and blew on it repeatedly. It gave forth very sweet music.

The rabbit took this special piece of bone and went home. He gave it to his son, Arouna, to use it as a toy. The little rabbit used the piece of bone and happily played around with his friends. All the animals who heard the song of the rabbit liked that piece of bone. The monkeys fell in love with the music it produced when Arouna blew on one end of it. They sat around Arouna and kept listening to the music. It was truly a work of art. They asked him to give them all a chance to play on it, too.

Baby rabbit would not let anyone even hold this precious musical instrument for long. He feared losing his favourite toy and therefore would grab it back very quickly whenever someone took it from him. Since the animals did not get a chance to use this wonder of music, they were not happy. The monkeys in particular wanted to play longer with the piece of bone. But they never got the chance.

One day, they made a plan to steal this treasure. They went to the little rabbit and told him, "Hey, little one, your father had told you to make two trips a day to the river to fetch water." Arouna had already done what his father had ordered him to. So, he told them that he had completed the task.

Then, the monkeys told him, "Hey, little one, your father had also asked you to cut firewood in the forest and bring two loads of it each day." Arouna again had completed the task. So, the monkeys did not get any chance to steal the piece of bone.

The monkeys thought of yet another plan. They went and told the little rabbit, "Hey, your father had asked you to take rest regularly and sleep two times a day." Arouna realized that he had slept only once. Not knowing that the monkeys were playing tricks on him he went to take his second nap. He put the pipe under his pillow and lay down to sleep.

The monkeys came to know where he had kept the pipe. They could not take it out because any little movement would wake up the baby rabbit. If he understood their real intentions, he might never obey them again. So, they collected some wild grass and put it on Arouna's eyes so that he could not see anything when he woke up. The monkeys then took the pipe and ran away.

Arouna could not open his eyes after his second nap and knew at once that the monkeys had played a trick on him. He searched for his toy but could not find it. He began to cry.

A bird came by and asked him why he was crying. He described how the monkeys had stolen his toy. The bird promised to help him. It told Arouna to fetch food for her children (chicks) while she would take care of his problem with the monkeys. Arouna took the basket the bird gave him and fetched worms, a special type of worms found on the bark of trees. He also collected roots of plants for himself. He filled one basket with worms for the birds and another with roots of plants. He then settled down to wait for the bird's return.

The bird went in search of the monkeys. When she finally found them, they were playing with the pipe. The bird watched for some time and then asked them to give her the pipe so that she too could give it a try. They refused to give it to her. At her insistence, the oldest monkey told them to give the bird a chance. The bird took the pipe and blew on it. "How nice it is", said the bird and returned it to the monkeys. The bird watched the monkeys again for a while.

Then she said, "Let me blow the pipe once more. I want to sit on the platform above the fireplace and blow on it one more time." Since she had returned the pipe peacefully the first time, they gave it to her.

Traditional fire place

Bamboo-shoot, seeds of vegetables, etc., are hung
above the fire to keep them dry

The third time the bird sat on the chimney and played
on the pipe. Then came the fourth time on the top of
the roof. She played one complete song and flew off with
the pipe in its beak. The monkeys ran after her, but they
could not catch her.

What you do to others, others can do to you!

IMMORTAL WIFE

◆ ◆ ◆

A rich man had two wives. The elder one was kind but the younger one was cruel. They lived separately not very far from each other. Both of them had children. The cruel woman was always jealous of the other woman. She was aggressive and wanted all good things for herself alone. Due to this, the elder woman who was kind could not have anything that was better than what the other woman had. However, she was calm and never fought back.

One day the two women decided to go to the river to gather crabs for their children. They set out together. Each of them took a basket to hold whatever they collected. The elder one gathered crabs, but the cruel woman collected only snakes. When their baskets were full, they started out on their return journey.

On their way back to the village, they came across some beautiful orchids. They were blooming on the top of a big, tall tree. The cruel woman said to the other, "Sister, let us get those beautiful flowers for our children." The elder woman replied, "They are, indeed, very beautiful. However, we cannot climb trees. How can we get to them?" The younger lady was adamant. She had cruel plans. She said, "I will not go home without some of those flowers. Please get them for me." The elder woman did not know how to climb trees. She protested, but the younger one insisted on having her way.

The kind, elder woman slowly climbed up the tree. She plucked the followers and dropped them down one by one saying, "This one is for your children and this is for my children." The cruel woman did not bother to collect the flowers. She opened her basket of snakes and released them. The snakes started climbing up the tree where the elder woman was. They bit the lady and she fell dead.

The cruel woman picked up the elder lady's basket of crabs and went home. The children of both women were waiting for their return. When they saw that the elder one did not return, they inquired, "Aunty, where is our mother?" She replied, "Your mother is a greedy woman. She is still collecting crabs, not caring about returning home." She then took out some crabs for them and said, "Cook these and have them until your mother returns."

The children took the crabs and cooked a meal. They waited for their mother but she never returned. That night, the eldest among them had a dream. She saw her mother in the form of a turtle. The turtle said to her, "I will meet you tomorrow at the pond when you come to get water."

The children went to the pond the next day. They found a turtle beneath a rock and took it home. They kept it inside an empty pot. The cruel lady heard about the turtle. She wanted to kill the turtle, too. She sent her children to the kind woman's house to find out whether the turtle was really there. One of the children said to the elder women's daughter, "I am feeling thirsty. Please give me some water." As she opened the pot, the child saw the turtle and asked for it. When they refused to give it to her, the child began to cry.

The elder woman's daughters were as kind and tender-hearted as their mother had been. They gave the turtle to the cruel lady's children. The children took it home and gave it to their mother. The cruel lady killed it and cooked a meal with it. Her husband, the rich man, came to know about it and refused to eat any of this food. He would not allow anyone else to eat it either. He took the entire pot and threw away the food in the garden.

A mustard plant grew up the next day at the spot where the food had fallen. The cruel woman saw the plant and plucked it. She cooked it and served it to her husband again. But her husband refused to eat this plate of mustard leaves either; he threw the whole food again at the back of the house. Next, a pumpkin plant grew out of the food thrown in the garden. Then, a chilly plant and from the chillies there grew a banyan tree.

They took the banyan tree's fruit to the kitchen and kept it above the fireplace. Whenever someone wanted to eat the fruit, they could not find a knife to cut it with. When they would finally find a knife, the fruit would have disappeared. No one ever got to eat the fruit.

The fruit later got transformed into a woman. She used to clean the house and pound paddy. The rich man saw her and remarried her. She was taken back to where her children were living.

Not long after, the cruel woman came to know about it. When the elder woman came to visit her, she instructed her children to ask her for the necklace she was wearing. So, the children said to her, "Let us try your necklace." The woman did not want to give it to them; but, kind as she was, she could not refuse the request of young children. She took it out and gave it to them saying, "Have a look at it and give it back to me after a while." It was getting late in the evening. The elder woman had to return home. But the children did not return her the necklace. She said to them, "Children, give me back my necklace. I need to go home."

The children, as instructed by their cruel mother, did not return the necklace in a proper way. They threw it under the bed. When the woman bent down to collect it, the cruel woman pushed her so that she fell down and died. However, that was not the end of the story. The elder woman's necklace transformed itself into a bird and flew away. The husband, the rich man, was not aware of this. He only knew that his wife was dead.

One day the man's servants came to the forest to gaze his horses. They heard a bird chirping. It said, "Tell my man! Tell my man! Else your horses will look as though starved no matter how much you feed them, or they will get hurt by a knife."

The servants did not take this warning seriously. They neglected to inform their master of what they had heard from the bird. Every day the bird met them and reminded them with its chirping. This went on for several days. True to what the bird had warned them, the horses became weaker and weaker day by day.

The rich man noticed that the horses were getting feeble and asked his servants, "What is wrong with my horses? Are you not feeding them regularly?" At this the soldiers suddenly remembered the message of the bird. They realized that it was not just the normal chirping of a bird. They told their master, "Sorry master, there was a bird who used to chirp whenever we went to gaze the horse. It wanted us to pass on a message about her to you. Else it warned us that the horses would look starved."

The man got suspicious. He guessed that the bird would be his wife again. He ordered his servants to bring it to him immediately. When the bird was brought, he put grains on his palm and said to the bird, "If you are my wife, eat this grain." The bird pecked at the grains eagerly and ate them. The rich man then took the bird home and kept it in a cage.

The bird had the heart of a kind human being. It loved the children and could understand things just as a human being could. One day the cruel woman saw the bird trying to remove some dirt from her child's eye. She immediately killed the bird and cooked it. This made her husband very sad again. He did not allow anyone to eat the food and threw it away in the garden. A big, tall tree grew out of it. The cruel woman was happy and thought the kind woman would not come back again in whatever form.

One day, there was a strong wind and many houses in the village collapsed under it. A king from the neighboring kingdom also lost his house in this storm. He needed a strong tree to use as the main pillar for his new house. He sent his soldiers to search for a suitable tree.

The soldiers saw the tree near the rich man's house, the tree that had grown up from the cooked bird that had been thrown away. They started preparations to cut it down. The kind woman's daughter saw them and prevented them from cutting the tree because she knew that it was her mother.

Despite her protests, the soldiers tried to cut the tree down. So, the girl said to them, "If you want this tree as a pillar for your king's house, tell him that he has to marry me." The soldiers went back and reported all that had happened. The king said to them, "Tell the girl that I will marry her. Cut the tree down and once it is down, tell her the king will not marry her."

The soldiers went to the girl the next day. They told her that the king had promised to marry her. So, she allowed them to cut the tree. Once the tree had fallen, the soldiers said, "The king will not marry you." As soon as she heard this the girl said to the tree, "Let my mother stand up again." The tree stood up and went back to being exactly as it was before it was cut.

The soldiers were amazed. They went back to the king and told him of all the latest events. The king suggested, "Tell her I will marry her. Then cut the tree and take it very far away from her house. Just before you cross the kingdom's borders, just tell her 'the king is not willing to marry you' and get away with the log."

The soldiers carried out the king's instructions. They cut the tree and took the log far away. As they were about to cross the border gate, they shouted, "The king will not marry you." The girl shouted back, "Let my mother stand up again." The log stood up and went back to where it stood before it was cut down.

There it stood in all its earlier glory, with its branches, leaves, fruits and flowers. When this news reached the king, he understood that he had no other option. He took the girl as his queen. They cut the tree and built a house with it. They lived happily ever after in the company of her mother permanently in their house.

ASHO AND MICHARUNG

The clever man and his foolish friend

◆ ◆ ◆

(The story of Asho and Micharung is about two men who lived in similar ways yet are very different from each other. They shared a brotherly relationship and helped each other in every sphere of life. They were different because one was 'clever' and the other was 'strong'. Asho, who was clever, used his intelligence to get what he wanted. He was cunning and tricked people to his advantage. Micharung was stupid and he survived only because of his physical strength. He tried to trick people as Asho did, but would always end up falling into the opponent's trap.)

Asho's mother conceived him by eating a fruit. This is how it took place. She lived with her brothers and was engaged to be married to a man very soon. One day she went to the field to take food and wine for her brothers who were at work. When she poured wine from the jug, a snake came out of it. They killed the snake and threw it away.

Her brothers sensed that what had happened was an omen and told their sister, "Do not go near the dead snake nor even look at it again." Since she did not know the reason for this restriction, she only grew curious about it. When her brothers returned to their work, she turned in the direction where the dead snake had been thrown.

She saw a ripe fruit lying there and found it very tempting. "It cannot be bad," she thought to herself and she ate it. This was how she came to conceive her child, and Asho was born to her.

Hearing about her pregnancy, her fiancé was hesitant to marry her. However, they loved each other so much that he was convinced that it could not be any other man's child. When she explained to him that the conception took place after she ate the fruit, he believed that there was something supernatural about the whole event and they should not interfere with it. He decided to go ahead with the marriage. In due course a son was born to the woman and they named him Asho.

Asho was very clever right from his childhood. When he was young, his father made a plan to kill him because he was not his own son. He took him to a hill slope and asked him to stand below a huge boulder. When he started to roll the boulder down so that it would crush him to death, the boy stretched out his hand and stopped the rock from moving towards him and said, "Daddy, Where shall I push this stone?" So, his plan to kill the young Asho failed.

He made a second attempt in a field. He started cutting a huge tree and asked the boy to stand in the direction where the tree was falling. The boy caught hold of the tree and asked, "Daddy, where do you want me to throw this log?" Asho understood that his father's intensions were bad. He decided to leave home.

He went into the wilderness and was looking for a place where he could settle down when he met Micharung.

Micharung was physically strong and a very daring man; but he was stupid. He would do stupid things precisely because he would pretend to know everything. *(Liangtuang is a person who has extraordinary physical strength. He uses his strength to help his people in the community.)*

From the moment they met, Micharung addressed Asho as 'elder brother'. Asho also treated him as his younger brother and they were close to each other. They did not have a house of their own. They moved from place to place and lived in caves and trees. They were friends to many animals, too, wherever they went. They knew how to communicate with them.

Asho's wife was wise and she would help her husband even in taking important decisions. However, Micharung's wife was no wiser than Micharung himself. She would do whatever her husband asked her to without rationalizing things on her own.

Tool making

One day Asho and Micharung planned to do some iron work for making tools. They went to Zeilat river, which is now in Tousem Sub-division of Manipur's Tamenglong district. They heated the iron and molded them into whichever shape they wanted.

The work involved a lot of continuous hammering of the red-hot iron. The king of the river was irritated by all this noise. He sent fishes from the river to deliver a message to Asho and Micharung. They insulted the fish and chased them away. The fishes went back under the water and informed their king of the poor reception they had received. After some time, a python came out of the water and shouted, "Who is disturbing the peace of my area? Why are you still here?"

The two men heard the python. Asho was scared and did not want to risk his life. He ran away to safety. Micharung stayed on. He was stupid, but he was strong. He pulled out a red-hot tong from the fire and caught the python with it. He took the python home.

Phiantu-bui (Magical spear)

The python requested them to set him free. Asho said to him, "We are not letting you off now. We will do whatever we want with you." The python was scared. He said to them, "If you release me, I will give you something that has magic power." "What is that?" they asked. The python replied, "I will give you a magical spear. You hold the spear, strike a stone or even the ground and ask for anything you want, and you will have it." They thought this was a better thing to have than a python. They agreed to the proposal. The python straightened itself out and took out the spear from inside its stomach. He gave them the spear and went away.

Once they had this magical spear, they were never short of anything. They would hit the stones and sand and ask for whatever they wanted. They built a house at a place called Machiang, equipped it through a wanton use of the magic spear and lived a comfortable life.

When they saw that they could really get whatever they wanted, they began to get greedy and selfish. They became very materialistic. The power of the spear made them lazy. Differences started to grow between them, and they became jealous of each other.

Farming

Since they had settled down and had their own house, they decided to start growing crops. Asho was the first one to make the move. One day he invited the people of the village to come and work in his field. He did not take any food packages for the workers but had only the magical spear with him. The people started grumbling that they would not be able to work till evening because they had seen him coming without any packages.

When it was time for lunch he went ahead of the others to the shelter where meals are usually prepared and served in the fields. He held the spear in his hand, hit it against a stone and asked for food and wine. The magic worked. Packages of food and gourds of wine appeared before him. He invited all those working in his field to come for their lunch. Everyone had their fill and then they resumed their work.

When Micharung came to know about it, he also wanted to follow the same procedure. He went to Asho's house to get the magical spear. Asho did not want Micharung to enjoy any longer the luxury of the magical spear. So, he made another spear which looked like the magical one and gave it to him.

Micharung was too stupid to see the difference. He took the spear and left for the field where he had invited many people from the village. He had told them not to bring lunch packages. He would feed them. The people were surprised to see him arrive in the field empty handed, except for his spear. They asked him how he intended feeding them. He replied, "Don't worry. I will arrange everything." When lunch time came, he took the spear and hit it against a stone. He asked for food and wine, but nothing happened.

When he looked at it carefully, he understood that it was not the magical spear. It made him very furious. From then on, he did not trust his brother the way he used to. Differences between them grew far worse.

Encounter with Traders

Inspite of the differences between them, Asho being the elder and a sensible man, always helped his younger brother in difficult situations. One day a group of traders (from the Meitei community of Manipur) happened to pass by. They usually bring with them items like soap, sweets, salt, sugar and other food items from the town and exchange them for chillies or fruits from the village. Since these things were not marketed in the village, they were highly valued.

Seeing what they were carrying, an idea struck Asho. He welcomed the guests and fed them with good food. At night, when they were fast asleep, he instructed his wife to warm up some water. They poured it on the guests to make it look as though they had urinated in bed. The next morning, when the guests woke up, Asho pretended to tidy up the bed they had used. He pointed to the wet bed and said, "I have been very hospitable to you. How could you wet my bed in return for my hospitality? You have to pay a heavy price for this." He took all their belongings and let them return empty handed.

When Micharung saw what his brother had acquired, he asked, "How did you manage to get so much wealth overnight without making any effort?" Asho replied, "When the traders from Imphal came with goods, I invited them to my house. I welcomed them and fed them with good food. When they were fast asleep, I asked my wife to warm up some water and pour it on them so that they would not wake up as they would if cold water were poured on them."

Before Asho could even complete the whole story, his brother said, "I know what to do now," and went home. That evening, when he saw some traders with goods, he invited them to his house. He fed them and did as his brother had described. However, since he had not listened to him properly, he did not perform the trick as his brother had done. He told his wife to boil water when the guests were asleep. He then poured the hot water on the guests. Feeling the heat, they woke up and got furious. They caught him and took him away with them.

On hearing the news, Asho went to rescue his brother. He asked the traders to release Micharung. But they were in no mood to do so. Asho thought of a plan. (The Meitei communities live mostly in the Imphal area of Manipur. One of their staple foods is fish). He said to the traders, "I know of a tree that bears fish." The traders could not believe what they heard. "How can a tree bear fish?" they asked. He took them to a place to prove himself and showed them a tree. Pointing to it he said, "This is the tree. You may climb and check it out for yourself." One of them climbed up and returned saying he could not find any fish. "You are a liar," they said. In order to convince them he said, "What if I can get you a tree that bears fish? You will have to give me whatever I ask for."

He climbed the tree and took out a small fish from his pocket when no one could see him. Returning to the ground he showed them the fish and said, "See it for yourself. I did find fish on this tree. There is lots more of it up there. You have to meet my demand." The traders were astonished to see him with the fish. But since they had promised to give what he asked for, they agreed to release Micharung on asho's demand.

Sometimes we land in serious trouble if we do not listen fully to what people have to say. Asho was clever and he would get what he wanted by making use of his tricks.

Such crooked ideas and tricks like those of Asho did exist even in the past. We do not emulate them. We do appreciate the love between the two brothers. Though Micharung never listened to Asho properly and got into trouble, Asho was always there by his side. Micharung in return looked up to him as to an elder brother and had full faith and trust in him.

Reformation

Asho realized later in life that his behavior was not of the best. He decided to reform himself. He did so by sharing all he had with the people around him. He started a 'dormitory' for girls (kailiu). There were seven girls who came regularly to the dormitory. He fed them and took care of them well. It was said that the young girls did not want to return to their own homes because of the warm hospitality they got from Asho.

Due to his kindness, one day god appeared to him and asked him to come to his kingdom in the West. He left his farm, his cattle and his family to enter the kingdom of god. When Asho was gone, the dormitory perished too. The girls felt left out not being associated with any dormitory. They therefore decided to go elsewhere. They told their parents not to look for them if they did not return. The girls later joined Asho in the kingdom in the West.

From then on, when Zeliangrongs look up to the night sky and see the constellation with seven stars, they say that they are the "girls from Asho's dormitory." All the animals left behind by Asho found their way to the jungle. His dogs too ran away, and they became the ancestors of our foxes. Till today the fox is known to the Zaliangrongs as "Asho's dog."

NOTHITHIAN

The Orphan beloved of all animals

Once upon a time, a long time ago, there lived in a small village of Bishnupur District in Manipur (India) a boy called Nothithian. He was an orphan. So, people in the village did not like him, though not for any particular fault of his. In those days all orphans used to be treated badly. Perhaps the mentality in those days was that the orphan was, somehow, responsible for the premature death of their parents.

Although people were unkind to him, there was something about him that attracted all the animals in the forest towards him. Whenever people in the village went hunting without Nothithian, they would not get any animals. It was not the same whenever he was there. The people noticed the difference, but no one knew what the reason was. They would make sure that he was with them whenever they went hunting.

After every hunt the villagers would cut up the animals they killed and share the meat equally among themselves. However, no matter how useful Nothithian was for them, they never gave him any good or fleshy parts of the animals. They would give him only the unwanted meat or the intestines of animals. Nothithian developed a dislike for the hunt and would try to avoid going with the villagers, but people would insist that he come along. They knew, if he was not with them, they would return home empty-handed.

One day, they all went hunting. They did not find any animals. Everyone asked Nothithian, "What is wrong today?" His friends were sitting silently on a huge branch of a tree. Nothithian turned to look at his friends and realized that the branch they were sitting on was not actually the branch of a tree, but a huge snake. Nothithian said to them, "Look at what you are sitting on. It is not a branch." Everyone saw that it was a huge snake. They killed the snake and cut its meat. As usual, they gave only the intestines to Nothithian. With no complaints whatever, although his desires were not met, he took the intestines and went to the river to clean them. He found a small drum within the intestine of the python. He did not tell anyone about it and took it home. He would beat the drum and all the animals and birds could hear him. They would come to him whenever he played on the drum and thus became very popular among the animals. The drum brought him luck, too.

The gods were always in favour of him. They felt that the villagers were not fair to Nothithian and decided to help him in a special way. One day, he had a dream in which he was told by a goddess to build a house (a Tarangkai). She also told him where the house was to be built and which tree he ought to use as its main pillar.

Women here are seen pounding rice – it is done as a
group activity on special occasions like the construction
of Tarangkai (Pic: Old Tamenglong, 1994)

(Tarangkai is a traditional house of the Rongmei Naga tribe. It cannot be built by just anyone, but by someone who has wealth, power and prestige. Permission for building the house is sought at the village council by throwing a tea party. Hence, all the villagers are involved in building a Tarangkai when permitted by the concerned heads. All of them are fed by the owner till the house-warming ceremony is completed. Women and unmarried girls cook and serve the men who do the construction work. It is built with just one middle pillar which should be very tall. The rest of the pillars are only support pillars and are as low as 3-4 ft from the ground. Pictures of animals and birds killed are painted on the front walls of the Tarangkai with the blood of these animals. The house-warming ceremony is marked by people dancing, playing games and young men displaying their skills/strength. The traditional wine (the rice wine) is served throughout the feast. Household chores are shared among men and women of the entire village.)

The day after he had the dream, Nothithian called his friends and went in search of the particular pillar tree. It was to be found on the bank of river Apin, situated near the present-day Loktak project area of Manipur. They searched everywhere but could not find it. When they happened to look into the water, they saw the reflection of the said tree. It was big and tall, and had a very straight trunk. They looked at the tree more closely before they searched again.

It was strange, for they could not find it anywhere around. They were anxious. "It must be the devil trying to play with us," one of them complained. They had lost all hope of locating the tree and began suggesting that they should go home before some evil befell them. Nothithian was unwilling to give up the search for the tree pointed out to him by the goddess. He wanted to find it there and then. But his friends were tired after a whole day's search for the tree. They all returned home. He had reluctantly to join his friends.

That night Nothithian had another dream. The gods asked him to offer an animal in sacrifice to them. He woke up the next day, killed a goat and offered it to the gods.

The making of a Tarangkai at Old Tamenglong, Manipur.
Men from the community pulling a log of wood for
the main pillar of the Tarangkai (pic 1994)

(In the old days, animals were offered as sacrifices to gods in order to get blessings from them. They would kill the animal by shedding its blood. The animals offered cannot be eaten nor taken back home. They would leave the animal in a place spe-

After the sacrifice, he went to the river again with his
friends. They looked into the water and saw the same
tree that they had seen the previous day. They looked
around, and this time they found the tree with a straight
trunk that had been described to Nothithian by the gods.
It stood tall on the bank of the river.

They cut the tree and carried the long trunk home. Then,
they began building the Tarangkai using the trunk as
the main pillar. When the construction was completed,
it became Nothithian's house. He was a poor boy, but
he somehow managed to build the Tarangkai which was
un-imaginable for a boy like him. Tarangkai symbolizes
power and wealth; and the gods had provided him with
whatever was required to complete the house. There
were celebrations with music and dance on completing
the Tarangkai, for Nothithian had earned the respect of
his village.

Dance troop at the making of the Tarangkai, Old
Tamenglong, Manipur (Pic 1994)

There was something extraordinary about the middle
pillar. After the house was completed different types of
birds made their nests on the roof. Varieties of bee built
their hives too. Nothithian became very prosperous and
that was evident to everyone in the village.

The people came to understand that it was the pillar
that made Nothithian rich. They began to be envious of
him. They justified their envy arguing that it was not fair
that only Nothithian to be rich because they were all in-

volved in bringing the pillar and building his Tarangkai. They wanted to get a share of his wealth. So, they decided to pull down the house and cut the pillar into pieces so as to distribute it among all those who were involved in bringing the pillar. They thought that everyone would become rich if they could get even a piece of it.

The people destroyed Nothithian's house and pulled down the pillar. But before they could cut it into pieces, it rolled down the hill and went back into the river from where it had been brought. It was actually not a real tree; it was in fact, a python. Thereafter the python would come to the village every night. It bore a hole from the river right through to the village. It would come into a small shed which was built exclusively for pounding paddy. Every morning, people found marks on the husks. It would be smoothened out by the movement of some animal. Though they were not sure what mark it was, they set a trap there.

A place for pounding paddy

A big python was caught in the trap the next day. Men in the village decided to kill it and share its flesh. They pulled the python out of its hole little at a time and kept cutting its flesh piece after piece. The meat was distributed to all the villagers. It is a practice to share the meat from a hunt among all the people of the village. There was a widow who lived all by herself in the same village. Her house was on the top of a hill, a little away from the rest.

Since the widow lived almost out of the village, she was the last one to receive her share of the python's flesh. By the time the men came with the meat, the widow was already asleep. They woke her up and told her that they had come to deliver the python's meat to her too. Since it was late, she did not want to get out of bed and come to the door. She told them to hang the meat on a pole just outside her house. It was the pole to which she used to tie her drying line for her wet clothes. The men hung the meat on that pole as directed by the widow and went away.

A little while after midnight, the widow heard loud thunder; the earth shook. She woke up and ran outside the house. She called out to the villagers, but no one answered. She wondered what might have caused the frightening disturbance, but it was too dark yet to see anything. Since everything seemed calm and quiet once again, she went back inside the house and returned to her bed.

The next morning, she came out to see what might have happened in the night. To her dismay, she found that the whole village was gone. It had disappeared totally. There had been a heavy landslide that started right under the pole where the meat of the python was hung. The python was evidently angry with the villagers and it had taken its revenge on them. It spared only the widow's house because she had not eaten its meat.

The whole village was carried away by the landslide into the river 'Apin'. The people were all dead and they were transformed into snakes and pythons. It is believed that some pythons and snakes are seen even now wearing earrings. These are the females who were among the people of the village who were transformed from humans into snakes and pythons when the great earthquake took place in that village.

REVENGE OF A MOTHER AND SON

Many years ago a mother lived in a village with her little son. The little boy loved to play with the children in the neighborhood; but, in the course of their games the children would say, "The little boy's grandfather will come and eat you up if you don't play well." This was bothering the little boy's peace of mind. He did not like what they said about his grandfather. He did not understand why people would talk about his grandfather in this wicked manner.

One day he went home and asked his mother where his father was. He told his mother what the other children would say about his grandfather and asked her what the reason was. His mother did not tell him anything. She told him that he was too young to know anything about his father and grandfather.

The mother promised him that she would tell him everything when he grew older. The little boy, however, could not wait that long. He kept thinking what could be wrong with his grandfather and what could have happened to his father.

He started asking his mother every day. He did not like the fact that all his friends had a father, but not he. However young he was, he knew there was something that was not quite as it should be. He had to get to the bottom of the matter immediately or he could not have any peace of mind. The little boy's mother did not want to tell him the truth; but, since the boy made it clear that he would not accept anymore delay, she was forced to tell him whatever had happened to his father.

His grandfather was a tiger. He used to live in the form of a human being. One day, when he was angry, he turned into a tiger and ate the boy's father. The mother had not wanted the little boy to know all this because he was still young. She had wanted him to understand this only when he would be big and strong enough to do something about it. As soon as he heard the story, he told his mother that he would go and take revenge for his father. His mother tried to stop him, but he would not stay back.

She cooked food for the boy and packed it in banana leaves. She made two packages: one for him to eat and the other with the bones of a chicken. She told him not to eat anything given by his grandfather because it would be the flesh of his father. He should take food only from the package she gave him. The package with bones was so that he could pretend to be eating what his grandfather gave. She told him specifically that his grandfather should not know that he was not taking the food he gave.

The little boy set out on his journey to take revenge on his grandfather. As he journeyed through the jungle he came across an ant. Seeing the boy, the ant asked, "Where are you going on such a hot day?" The boy answered that he was on his way to have vengeance for his father. The ant asked him if it could ride on his shoulder till he reached its destination. The boy helped the ant and the ant, in return, blessed the boy.

As he proceeded, he met a grasshopper. Its wings had got stuck in a bush. When the boy came along, it asked the boy, "Where are you going on such a sunny day?" The boy answered, "I am going to take revenge for my father." The grasshopper asked him for his help. The boy helped to free its wings from the thorny bush. The grasshopper also thanked and blessed the boy.

The boy kept going and soon came across a sparrow. Some fruit was stuck up in its beak. The sparrow asked the boy, "Where are you going on such a sunny day?" The boy replied, "I am going to take revenge for my father." The sparrow requested the boy to help remove the piece of fruit that was stuck in its beak. When it was removed, the sparrow blessed the boy.

It was a long journey. But he did not stop anywhere. He

came across some elm trees (*Elms trees produce slippery gel when cut. This gel was used as a hair conditioner in the old days. Women would cut its branches and store them. They used it when washing their hair to make it soft and silky.*) The boy cut many branches from the elms and left them lying on the road. Then he cut branches from other trees, too, and made arrows for his bow. He left his bow and the arrows on a tree and proceeded with his journey toward his grandfather's house.

When he reached there, his grandfather gave him a warm welcome. He told him that he was very happy to see him after such a long time. In order to celebrate his arrival, he promised to kill some fattened cattle. The grandfather sent one of his cattle to the jungle and told it not to return until it was called back. He wanted to give the little boy the impression that he had killed the cattle. He then cooked the flesh of the boy's father.

When the meal was served the boy followed the instructions given to him by his mother. He pretended to take the meal, and quietly ate from his own food packet. His grandfather said, "Son, eat well for you will be with me only a few days." The boy replied, "Thank you, grandfather, for your generosity. You have treated me well." He left the bones from his mother's packet as though they were from the meat given by his grandfather.

The grandfather had plans to eat the boy when he fell asleep. When night came, he said, "Son, you must be tired after a long journey. Take a good rest." However, the boy tried his best to remain awake. Every now and then the grandfather would check whether he was asleep. "Son, are you awake?" he would ask. The boy kept answering him each time he was called. This went on till dawn; so he could not kill the boy.

The next day too, the little boy stayed awake the whole night. On the third day, he told his grandfather that he was returning home. His grandfather requested him to stay longer since he had not yet got the chance to kill him. Saying that his mother would be eagerly waiting for him, the boy bade farewell to him.

The grandfather wanted to make his last attempt at eating the boy. He pretended that he wanted to drop his son a part of the way. He took his dog along and accompanied the boy. After walking some distance, he bade his final goodbye and turned back. He then asked his dog to chase the little boy. As ordered by its master, the dog barked and chased the boy. The boy ran as fast as he could. When he looked back, he saw a huge tiger running towards him. It was his grandfather. He had been waiting for the boy for a long time, but had never got the right opportunity to eat him.

The boy managed to reach the place where he had cut down branches of elm trees and scattered them all over. Since the ground was slippery, the tiger and the dog could not run fast. The boy climbed the tree where he had left his bow and arrows and shot the tiger several times. The tiger fell to the ground, but the boy could not come down till he was sure that the tiger was really dead.

A bear happened to come by. The boy asked the bear to find out whether the tiger was dead. He was afraid. He said that if the tiger was not dead, it might wake up and kill him. So he could not do the job. He shook his head and walked off.

The boy was sad. It was getting dark and he was hungry. He thought of his mother. He knew she would be waiting for him eagerly. The ant passed by and asked him, "Why are you sad, my friend?" The boy told him what had happened. He requested the ant to help him by checking whether the tiger was dead. The ant climbed on the tiger's body and checked if his legs and tail were moving. However, it could not go around and check the whole body. "The legs and tail are no longer moving," said the ant and it went away.

The boy did not want to get down from the tree until he was sure of everything. He could not assume that the tiger was dead only because the legs and tail were not moving. He did not budge from where he was sitting.

The grasshopper came along. "Why are you sad, my friend?" it asked the boy. The boy told him everything and requested his help. It went around the tiger's body and said, "The body is no longer moving. I do not have the courage to check its head."

By then, the boy almost lost hope of getting home alive. But since he had been kind to all the animals he met, god did not abandon him in his distress. The sparrow appeared. It asked the boy why he was sad and offered to help him. The boy asked the sparrow to check whether the tiger was still breathing. Though it was scared, the sparrow could not refuse the boy. It flew round the tiger's head and confirmed that the tiger was not breathing anymore. The boy came down from the tree with his spear. He cut the tiger's throat and took its head with him. He wanted to show it to his mother as proof that he had avenged his father.

Meanwhile, during the three days the boy was away, the children in the neighborhood would disturb the boy's mother by knocking on her door. They would pretend to be the little boy and ask her to open the door. When she opened it in all eagerness to have her son back, they would giggle and run away. They kept repeating this several times. She finally decided she would never open the door any more for anyone again except for her son.

By the time the son reached home with the tiger's head, it was midnight. His mother was already asleep. He knocked on her door and asked his mother to let him in. She thought it was once again the little children having fun at her expense in the middle of the night. She did not open the door.

The boy hung the tiger's head just in front of the door and told her, "Mother, it is your own son. I have avenged my father. I am keeping the tiger's head here at your door to prove that it is me." He went to sleep in the barn just behind the house. He was sad. He looked at the stars and tears rolled down his cheeks. The angels felt pity for the little boy and they took him with them.

His mother opened the door the next day. She had forgotten what her son had told her in the middle of the night about the tiger's head at her door. When she saw it unexpectedly, she had such a great shock that she died.

A barn - where harvest is stored

SELFISH INTENTIONS

◆ ◆ ◆

Once upon a time there lived a young girl. She was not an ordinary girl. She was unusually beautiful unlike the other girls of her age in the village. As was the custom in those days, young boys and girls would always be together, be it for work or social life. Life was full of fun at their age.

Men and women share work in the farms

The beautiful girl was especially fond of a particular boy. She was an aggressive young lady, self-confident, and always demanding exactly what she wanted. The boy did not fall for her beauty and did not respond to her. He was in love with another girl. She was a simple girl and was not exceptionally beautiful. It was her kind heartedness and simplicity that attracted him. The beautiful girl did not like this. She could not stand the fact that the boy she loved was interested in someone else. She tried every possible trick in her armory to win the boy over. However, she never succeeded. She waited for a day when she could have her revenge on the other girl.

Chores are carried out jointly, also because the
Nagas have strong sense of community

Boys and girls used do most of their daily chores together. They would go to bathe in the river, gather food from the forest, collect firewood, fetch drinking water and work in each other's field, always in groups, always together. Preparation for festivities in the community was done collectively.

One fine day, the boy's girlfriend fell ill. She could not join the others for work. She requested her lover to stay with her for the day. It was a cloudy day. The beautiful girl thought she would try to separate the boy from her rival and create an opportunity for herself to spend time with him. She thought of a plan and invited her friends to come with her to the forest. "Let us go and gather food today," she said. "It is not a good day for that," the boy replied. The others joined the boy and said, "The weather is not good. Besides, we cannot go when our friend is not well. We shall go when she gets well."

The jealous girl had made up her mind and she was used to getting her way always. She refused to give in. "What difference does it make if just one girl is not there? We will all go and be back early," she said.

Seeing her so adamant, her friends agreed to go along with her. They took their baskets and knives and set off for the woods. It was an unpleasant day. The weather was gloomy and everyone was not in the best of moods. They missed their friend who had been left behind. Only the beautiful girl was happy. She was sure that she could do something to get the boy she loved. "No other day could be as right as today," she said to herself.

They collected bamboo shoots, edible leaves, flowers, banana leaves and stem. The boy did his work as fast as he could and soon had his basket full. His mind was always on his girlfriend and he wanted to get back home early.

The beautiful girl would not leave any possibility for the boy to go off alone by himself. She inspected the boy's basket and pulled out whatever he had gathered. "What have you collected? They are not of good quality. You can get better ones," she said and chopped up everything in pieces.

The boy again quickly gathered a full basket of eatables. The girl inspected his basket again, throwing out everything. This went on till it was getting dark and it was time for them to go home.

In the meantime, back in the village the girl's illness became serious. She called out for her friend, but there was no one to pass on the message to the boy because all the youngsters had gone to the woods. She waited for evening to fall so that she could see her beloved, but he was too late. She breathed her last before he reached back home.

It was late in the evening when the youngsters got home. They saw many people in the village returning from a funeral. On inquiring, the boy came to know it had been the funeral of his beloved. He was angry with himself for not having spent time with his love. His only thought was, "Had I listened to my love, I would have been at her side at least on her last day!"

PRETTIER THAN QUEENS

◆ ◆ ◆

Once upon a time there was a king. One day he asked his soldiers to go hunting. The soldiers obeyed. They went to the jungle to carry out the king's order. In the evening, they returned empty handed, without a single animal. The king asked them, "What happened to you, dear men? Why have you not brought me any animal for my table?" They replied, "Master, we did not find any animals today. We will try again tomorrow."

The next day they went to the forests once more. There was no change. They came back empty handed. When the king asked them about it, they gave him the same reply. This went on for several days. But the soldiers never told the king what exactly was happening whenever they went into the jungle.

An extraordinarily beautiful woman lived in the jungle. She was a witch. Whenever the soldiers came to the jungle, she would attract their attention. They could not resist her charm. They would spend the entire day admiring her. There was something so magical about her radiance that the soldiers would completely forget the order of their king. They thought nothing of defying the king's order just to gaze at the woman.

After many days of not fulfilling their duty, the king

could recognize a change in the behavior of his soldiers. This was the first time they showed no sense of guilt for not performing their duties. The king began to doubt that the soldiers were telling him the truth. He called them and asked them, "My soldiers, tell me the truth about what is going on with all of you. Why have you not brought any animals till now after so many days of going on the hunt?"

They revealed the truth to him and said, "Master, whenever we go hunting, we see a beautiful woman. She has long wavy hair which she combs in front of us. She is so beautiful that we cannot take our eyes off her. As long as she is there for us to look at, we cannot go after any animals."

The king could not believe what he had heard. He said to himself, "No other woman could be more beautiful than my queens." He decided to challenge them, "Is she more beautiful than my eight queens?" he asked. "Yes master, she is more beautiful than your queens," the soldiers replied. The king was horrified. He did not like the suggestion that someone could be more beautiful than his queens. He asked his soldiers again to be certain that he was hearing them right, "Are you claiming that she is more beautiful than my queens?" "Yes Master," they answered, "much more beautiful!"

The king made a quick decision. He said to his soldiers, "Tell the woman that I will marry her." The soldiers went and gave the king's message to the woman. The woman replied, "Your king will not be able to satisfy my desires and wishes. I do not accept his proposal."

The woman's refusal of his proposal was conveyed to the king. The king felt insulted that someone could turn down his proposal for marriage. This made him even more adamant. He wanted to have the most beautiful woman as his queen. He sent his soldiers again with the message that he would fulfil every single desire and wish of hers if she would agree to become his wife. "Go right now and do not return without the woman," the king said to them. They went and told the woman, "The king promised to fulfil all your wishes and desires if you marry him." Hearing them, she agreed to the king's proposal. She was then taken to the palace.

The king saw her and was overwhelmed by the beauty of the woman. He took her inside to meet his eight beautiful queens. However, not everything was fine after the arrival of the witch. She pretended to fall ill. She complained of stomach pain as soon as she saw the queens. The best doctors were called to check what was wrong with the witch. No one could diagnose her illness. Some of them walked away saying that she was pretending. When no doctor prescribed any medicine for her, she said, "I will be fine if I boil the eyeballs of the eight queens and drink the water."

The king was stunned to hear this, but did not want to break his promise of fulfilling her wishes. The eyes of all the queens were pulled out and put into boiling water. While drinking the water, the witch swallowed the eye of the youngest of the queens.

The queens were now blind and they were a burden in the palace. The witch turned them all out. They found their way to the jungle and lived there. The youngest among the queens was pregnant at the time. While they lived in the jungle away from the palace, the time came for her delivery.

The imps in the jungle came to know that there were human beings living in the jungle. So, they came to see them and found that the youngest woman was about to deliver a child. The imps took pity on her and helped the woman in the delivery. A son was born to her. The imps loved the baby boy dearly. They took good care of the mother and the child. With the help of the imps, the boy grew up to be very clever.

The boy loved all the queens very much. He treated them equally as his own mother and took good care of them all. He would go to the palace, gamble, win and earn good food. When he brought the food to the queens, they refused to eat it thinking that he had stolen it from somewhere. The boy told them how he got it by winning at gambling. This continued for many years. No one knew much about the boy until he grew to be very handsome and wise. He became an adult within no time and became very well known to everyone in the kingdom. People inquired about him and found out that he was a prince. The witch also came to hear of it and wanted to kill him.

She made a plan and wrote a letter to her aunt who also lived in the jungle. She asked the prince to deliver the letter to her aunt. Not knowing that the letter was a plot for his own death, he took it and went into the jungle to find the queen's aunt. As he was walking, he came to a spot where several paths crossed each other. He was confused as to which one to take. As it was getting late and he had absolutely no idea which direction to follow, he decided to spend that night there, right where all these footpaths met.

The imps sensed that there was a human being nearby and came to where the boy was. They searched his pockets to check if they could find anything. "Human beings are complicated. Search him thoroughly," one imp suggested. From one of his inner pockets, the imps found the witch's letter. The letter said, "Dear aunt, do not let this boy live. Eat him up before he creates trouble for us." When they read this, the imps understood that he was the boy they had helped. They said to one another, "This boy cannot die. He is our son. We must do something to prevent him from getting killed."

They tore up the witch's letter and wrote another letter which said, "Dear aunt, please marry this boy and help him in whatever way possible." Then they put the letter back in the prince's pocket and woke him up. They instructed him what he had to do and showed him the right way.

The prince went in the direction they had pointed out. When he reached the house of the witch's aunt, he handed the letter over to her. She was overwhelmed by the thoughtfulness of her niece in sending such a handsome young man to her as a messenger. She read the letter and married the prince. She did not hesitate to carry out whatever he asked for. As he had been directed by the imps, he inquired how he could restore the eyesight of the eight blind queens. He also inquired how he could get back the missing eye of the youngest queen; the eye that had been swallowed by the witch.

He pretended to love the lady very much and said to her, "I want to see your heart. It must be as beautiful as you are." Not knowing his intensions, the lady spoke to him openly. "I never keep my heart with me. I take it out and hang it near the bed. This way, I don't have to feel sad and sorry for anything I do," said the lady. She showed the prince where her heart was kept. The youngest queen's eye was also hung alongside. He knew that if he took the heart, she could be killed.

The prince waited for the right moment to get the heart and the eye and escape from there. He stayed awake every night waiting for the lady to fall asleep. But a suitable moment never came. She would never sleep. One day, he gave the lady some wine and made her drunk. That, finally, made her fall asleep. The prince took the eye of his mother and the heart of the woman and ran away.

The witch's aunt woke up and got to know what the prince had done. She ran after him to get her heart and the queen's eye back. Seeing her behind him, the prince took out the heart, threw it to the ground and stomped on it with all the force he could muster. The lady at once fell down and died. The prince then returned to the palace and killed the witch too. He restored the sight of the eight queens and brought them back to the palace.

The king was overjoyed with the courage of his son. He felt sorry for his own stupidity of being bedazzled by a woman's bewitching charms. Not long after, the courageous prince was given the throne. He ruled wisely and justly for many years.

www.ingramcontent.com/pod-product-compliance
Lightning Source LLC
LaVergne TN
LVHW051518170726
843492LV00006B/1577